AGE OF WOLVES

FATED SERIES BOOK ONE

MARIAH STONE

Stone
Publishing

GET A FREE MARIAH STONE BOOK!

Join Mariah's mailing list to be the first to know of new releases, free books, special prices, and other author giveaways.

freehistoricalromancebooks.com

ALSO BY MARIAH STONE

Mariah's Time travel Romance Series

- CALLED BY A HIGHLANDER
- CALLED BY A VIKING
- CALLED BY A PIRATE
- FATED

Mariah's Regency Romance Series

- DUKES AND SECRETS

View all of Mariah's Books in Reading Order

Scan the QR code for the complete list of Mariah's ebooks, paperbacks, and audiobooks in reading order.

I would rather spend one lifetime with you than face all the ages of this world alone.

    — J.R.R. Tolkien

PROLOGUE

Lomdalen, Norway, 894

THE DOOR to the mead hall opened, daylight casting the thin, cloaked figure there in shadow.

"Is the king here?"

The figure's voice wasn't loud, but like a strong wind rippling the still surface of the fjord, it silenced the great hall swarming with guests.

A crawling sensation of threat had Ulf Hakonson reaching for the sword that lay on the bench by his side.

It was hard to see above the heads of dozens of tall warriors. Despite the daylight pouring into the hall from the entrance gate, oil lamps hung from wooden pillars bearing carvings of dragons, wolves, and serpents, illuminating somber, battle-clad faces. The scent of wood smoke, mead, cooked vegetables, and grilled meat masked the odor of many bodies packed inside the closed space.

King Harald, tall and broad, with a bear hide on his shoulders, rose from the table of honor at the far end of the hall, wiping mead from his long red beard. "The king is here."

Seven dozen of King Harald's men turned their heads to their leader, who stood next to Ulf's father, Jarl Hakon, a tall, muscular Viking with a birthmark covering his left eye. From Hakon's other side, Ulf's mother, Mia, grabbed her husband's large biceps, her face pale.

The thin figure walked down the aisle towards the table of honor, her white fur cloak sweeping over the floor reeds. Silence covered the crowd in her wake like an invisible blanket. Her staff thunked against the floor. With her face hidden in the shadows under her hood, it was impossible to say how old she was or how she looked.

Ulf's brother, John, rose, trying to see between the broad shoulders of the Viking warriors. "Who is that?"

Mia, Ulf's sister, named after their mother, jabbed her elbow into John's side. "Sit down! Are you blind? Do you not see her cloak is made of catskins?"

John sat down. "Oh..."

The witch. The seeress.

Völva.

As she approached the table of honor, an impulse to stop the seeress pulled at Ulf's gut, but offending a völva meant offending the gods.

John shifted the piece of roasted deer on the trencher with his eating knife. "Do you think it has anything to do with today, brother?"

Right. Today Ulf was eighteen. The last day when he could make his choice.

Ulf fingered an indent in the hard wood of the table. "No. I made my decision a long time ago."

His sister, only one year younger than him, threw a worried glance at him. Mother locked her panicked gaze on him through the crowd. They all remembered a night nine winters ago, when three Norns had appeared at a feast and forever changed Ulf's life.

The Norns were the mythical fates that defined all lives and destinies across time. One of them had sent Ulf's mother from the year 2019 to the year 875 while she had been pregnant with him. His mother had negotiated with the Norn, who had agreed that he could one day choose if he wanted to live in the twenty-first century or remain in the Viking Age. That day had come.

King Harald leaned against the table with his enormous arms bulging. Heavy silver chains rocked forward from his neck. "Do you bring word of the gods to me, honorable völva?"

The witch gave a slow nod, the white fur with black spots glistening in the firelight. "The gods sent me a vision." Her voice was still low but traveled around the great hall as though carried by the wind into every ear. "I have been seeking you these past twelve moons."

The pale-blue tattoos on one side of the king's face straightened as his expression became serious. "You found me."

Jarl Hakon exchanged a loaded glance with his wife.

Ulf's mother smiled at the hooded figure. "Would you like a bite to eat, völva?"

The witch cocked her head. "Ah. It is you. The woman who crossed time."

Hakon stood up so fast, his heavy wooden chair fell back with a crack. "By Odin, how do you know?"

Ulf's fist clenched around his sword. His sister put her hand on his shoulder. "Easy, Channing."

Channing was the nickname his mother used when she spoke English to him. It meant the same in the Celtic language as Ulf did in Old Norse. Wolf. She called him Channing to remind him of his roots.

Eirik, Ulf's best friend, leaned over to him. "What is going on?"

But Ulf was hanging on to every word spoken at the table of honor. The witch moved her staff to the left and to the right and the tiny mouse and bat skulls hanging from it rattled. "The Norns told me everything, Jarl Hakon. Everything."

At the mention of the Norns, his mother swung her gaze back to Ulf, and a shudder went through him.

King Harald chuckled. "Crossed time? I heard rumors but always thought people made up stories because of your legendary healing skills."

The witch raised her head. "What I must tell the king cannot wait."

Why was Mother shaking? Her forehead glistened under her beautiful hairdo; a straight line separated her strawberry blond hair in the middle, and a braid went around her head like a golden crown.

King Harald nodded and leaned over the table, closer to the völva. "No one respects the true gods more than I do. What did you see?"

She didn't reply. Instead, she looked over her shoulder in Ulf's direction. A chill, like the tip of an icicle was being dragged down his spine, went through him.

The völva turned back to King Harald and took one last step towards the table. The skulls clunked as she leaned towards the king, their heads almost touching.

Time slowed down, every beat of his heart loud in his ears.

His mother mouthed one word to him.

Run.

King Harald straightened up and unsheathed his sword with a loud swoosh of metal.

His bushy red eyebrows knit together. There was one thing in his hard stare.

Death.

"Kill Ulf Hakonson!" The king's voice sounded around the hall like a war horn, and a hundred pairs of eyes fell on Ulf.

Ulf scrambled across the bench and jumped to his feet, sword lifted.

Jarl Hakon unsheathed his own sword. "Protect my son!"

Both Harald's and his father's warriors hesitated. They'd been allies for years, drinking mead, sharing loot and treasure. Most importantly, they had fought together to put King Harald on the throne.

And now, to kill the son of a jarl? Spill the blood of their host's kin? That went against the Norse law of hospitality.

And why—because a woman in a catskin cloak had whispered something to the king?

"Kill him!" roared King Harald.

His men echoed him. The battle cry was thick and loud in Ulf's ears. Somehow Hakon had made it to his side and yanked him back by his collar.

The battle began.

An ax flew in Ulf's direction. A cold swoosh of air tickled the side of his head as it bit into his ear and cut a lock of his dark-blond hair. With a thunk, it hit the wall behind him.

Someone was pushing him.

Mother. "You need to go, Channing!" she said in English, trying to move him towards the gate.

"Go where?" Ulf cried.

"You know where, Channing. It's the only place he won't reach you."

Only it wasn't a place.

It was a time.

The future.

A rune stone stood in the sacred grove, raised in honor of the Norns. It would take him to the future if he chose.

Swords and axes clashed as the warriors fought. The room was full of grunts and yells of pain.

Ulf held his sword tighter. "No. You know my decision."

A warrior scythed his ax, and Mother deflected his attacks with her scramasax. Men now lay around them, dead and wounded. His father fought King Harald, who threw furious glances at Ulf. His sister and even his fifteen-year-old brother were fighting with grown men.

They were all protecting him. They could all die because of King Harald's whim.

They didn't need to die.

The king wanted to kill only Ulf.

So he'd challenge King Harald and finish this before anyone else was hurt.

Pushing the man off his mother, he darted towards the entrance gate. "Hey! Harald, you dirty cocksucker," he yelled. King Harald's face reddened, and he delivered a punch to Hakon's jaw. "You want me, come and get me!" Ulf pushed away another man and kept moving towards the gate. "Come on!"

"Get him!" roared Harald as he fought his way through the mead hall.

Ulf ran into the gray daylight of a Norwegian summer, looking around. From behind him, warriors spilled out of the mead hall, screaming, roaring, still in battle rage. Wheat-haired Eirik followed him.

Eirik whirled around and slashed at a warrior, then cried over his shoulder, "I have your back, brother! Go!"

Eirik had had his back so often; in every battle they'd stood shoulder to shoulder. He'd saved Ulf's life countless times. Odin's feet, he was thankful to have his family and friends. Risking their lives for him, always by his side.

He wouldn't be the cause of their deaths.

He gathered in as much air as his lungs could hold and let it out in a single, long roar. Everyone froze, and King Harald stopped at the gate, staring at him. There was a deep, bleeding gash on Harald's cheek.

Ulf hit his chest with his fist above where his heart was. "You want me? Come and get me. Leave my family alone."

He ran.

The village flashed by him as his feet pounded against the dirt-packed streets: timber longhouses with thatched roofs, fences, racks of drying fish, and smokers for meat. The village lay by the fjord, mountains rising like walls all around them. He ran uphill, following the path into the woods of the nearest mountain. Angry yells sounded behind him, then reduced to the soft pounding and rustling of many feet on the dirt path.

Soon, his lungs were burning, despite his good physical form. Behind him, tunics flashed between trees and bushes, blades of swords and axes glistened in the dull light.

He didn't know how long he ran, but when the woods cleared into a small grove, he stopped, panting, sweaty.

There it was, the rune stone that had brought his mother, pregnant with him, here from the twenty-first century.

The piece of granite reached his waist, bearing Norse runes and wavy patterns—it could be his escape.

Branches cracked behind him, and he turned back. There they were. King Harald, like a large red-maned bear, panting, sweat and blood mixed on his face. His father and his mother, who was holding on to Hakon. Everyone was breathing hard, exhausted from the long run up the hill.

"What are you waiting for?" cried his mother in English. "Go, Channing!"

He met King Harald's eyes. "No. No one will chase me away from my home and my family."

King Harald took his sword with both hands and positioned it on his shoulder. "You have nowhere to go, anyway."

If this would be Ulf's last day, so be it. He'd die protecting his family and meet his death with honor. With his sword in his hand, on a battlefield. He'd go to Valhalla.

But before he could launch at his enemy, something flashed in his side vision. As more warriors arrived at the sacred grove, everyone went still, staring at the rune stone. When Ulf glanced there, he couldn't move, either.

By the granite stone stood someone he'd never wanted to see again. An old lady who, together with her two sisters, had come into another mead hall nine years ago and had forever changed his life.

The Norn.

"No..." Ulf whispered.

Her eyes, icy blue, piercing and as old as time, held him. The rune stone stood beside her, dark and menacing.

His mother was shaking her head, covering her mouth. "Go, Channing..."

King Harald's eyes were darting between Ulf and the old lady. "Go where?"

The Norn Skuld, the one Ulf's mother had negotiated with, cocked her head. "My sisters were against this. But I am giving you your very last chance, Ulf Hakonson." She stretched out her hand to him and opened her palm. There it was, the golden spindle engraved with runes and patterns of leaves, serpents, dragons, and wolves. Sunlight shone on the spindle, blinding him. "Go."

Harald roared and ran at Ulf, but Hakon grabbed him by his red tunic and slashed his sword across. The king barely deflected the weapon with his own. The battle between the king's men and Hakon's men started again. The king tried to run at Ulf, but Hakon kept attacking him to distract him.

"I do not want to kill you, Hakon," roared Harald, "but if you keep trying to stop me, I will have to."

With horror, Ulf saw that now Harald's sword strikes turned to murderous. He aimed for his father's neck and head, like any warrior would—intending to end a life.

Eirik, wounded in his right shoulder, fought, holding the sword in his left hand. Ulf's sister, Mia, backed up against a tree, deflecting the strikes of a warrior's ax. John, who had never even been on a raid, fought a warrior twice his size...and was losing.

They were about to lose their lives because of him.

Even if he went back to the fjord and stole a boat, King Harald would find him and kill him. He was the most powerful man in Scandinavia.

Worse, he'd harm Ulf's family to get to him.

The Norn gave him a sad smile.

But how could he abandon them? Wasn't this an escape, an act of cowardice? This was not how his father had taught him to live. He had never run from a fight.

Just as Ulf's fist tightened around his sword, he saw it. Harald's arm, high in the air, sword raised for the deadly strike, aiming for his father's neck.

Ulf could never reach Hakon in time to protect him.

All he could do was distract Harald—and be gone.

Then this fight would be over.

"Harald, you piss-covered pig's cock!" he roared as he reached for the golden spindle in the Norn's hand.

The king turned to him, his face a mask of battle rage.

That was all Ulf needed to give Hakon a chance. With a last glance at his mother, he wrapped his fingers around the spindle's cool, smooth surface.

And everything went dark.

Ulf blinked as bright light stung his eyelids. The ground

beneath him felt too hard somehow. Squinting his eyes open, he scrambled to his feet, holding his sword at the ready.

But there were no blades, no blood, and no Vikings.

People jumped away from him. Men wore straight, narrow blue trousers, and tunics of various colors. Strangely, some women wore trousers, too, and many were in skirts so short they exposed their legs. Buildings of red, perfectly rectangular rocks and mortar, as well as gray, smooth stone, surrounded him—and they had windows, something he'd only seen in the British Isles, and only in the richest houses. It smelled like the sea, but also like burned metal and dust and something tart and bitter. Seagulls squawked over his head, and there was so much noise.

He looked over his shoulder and saw the sea and the port, with many beautiful white ships, white masts shooting into the sky, though some of them had no masts at all.

It had worked, he realized. He was in the future.

His stomach dropped. He lowered his sword. Where was he?

He came to a group of young men who were staring at him, both amused and scared. They tensed and all took a barely noticeable step back.

"What year is this?" he asked, marveling at how his mouth produced English with no effort.

One of them, with a smooth face and a short haircut, looked around with a shy grin. "Is this some sort of hidden camera thing? It's 2007, dude."

Two thousand seven... Why had the Norn sent him twelve years before his birth? His mother had traveled in time from Boston, so...

"Is this Boston?" he asked.

"Yeah, man."

Odin's arse. Boston...the place where his mother would meet his biological father, Daniel Esposito, in 2017. Where she'd get pregnant with him in 2019, then meet one of the Norns and travel back in time to ninth-century Scandinavia.

The place he'd need to make his home. No. He couldn't stay here. He had to find a way to get back to his family, to his friends. A way to protect them all from Harald and whatever madness the völva had instilled in him.

He wouldn't give up everything and everyone he cared about.

ONE

Boston, October 2021

"ELLA, WATCH OUT!" her partner screamed.

She swerved to the right.

The silver SUV with dark windows had swooped into the lane before her like a bird, and Ella had barely managed to avoid a collision. But now she'd overcorrected and was heading into the crowd of protestors walking down the sidewalk.

She slammed on the brakes, and the car squealed to a halt. The seat belt bit painfully into her chest, and Ricardo pressed both hands against the airbag panel, grunting a curse.

"Hey!" A man slammed at her bumper with a cardboard sign reading "Brothers Stop Killing Brothers!" and it broke in two. "What the hell, you're a cop!"

The whole scene had that surreal quality of the dreams she sometimes had. The blurring of reality around her. The crisp reflection of the sky in the glass high-rise and the windows of the brick and concrete office buildings bled like ink dropped in water. The protestors marching past and the cars driving on the opposite side of the street slowed to an unnatural crawl. Her fingertips tingled, and she felt like she could stop the event, pause it, rewind it or fast-forward.

Change things.

She shook off the sensation.

Breathing heavily, Ella rolled down her window. "Sorry!"

The uncharacteristically chilly October air cooled her heated cheeks. Her breath rushed out in a cloud.

Her partner, Ricardo, leaned closer to her. "You all right?"

The protestor shook his head and resumed marching along with dozens of other activists. Men and women of all ages strode past closed coffeehouses, a boarded-up art shop, and a security guard who'd walked out of a brownish-pink office building. Their gloved fists pumped in the air as they chanted out their pain. Many of them were likely unemployed and possibly even homeless. Several had dirty and patched coats and carried full backpacks.

Ella's eyes scanned the wooden sticks some of the banners were attached to. Those could become weapons later if things escalated. How many of them had hidden guns? Were the police already waiting by city hall or wherever these folks were heading? Under normal circumstances, there would have been officers posted to control the protest. But there simply weren't enough police to manage the growing number of demon-strations.

Ella let out a cleansing breath. "What is it with people today?"

Ricardo shifted in his seat and raised Ella's orange travel mug that he had held close to his barrel-like belly. "I don't know, but I have two good pieces of news for you."

With her heart still pumping hard, Ella twisted in her seat to look in the rear window. There was one car behind her, and it stopped to let her back up. She switched into reverse and slowly drove back onto the road. "Is one of them that the jerk in the silver SUV didn't make you spill my coffee?"

Soft snow began falling from the leaden sky, drifting down between the tall buildings of downtown Boston. Snow in October? Well, that was climate change for you.

Ricardo did a salute with the cup. "Yeah, that's one." He took a sip and exhaled with satisfaction. "Your dad makes the best coffee."

Ella braked and waved to the driver of the car to thank them for letting her in. "What's the other one?"

"The asshole that cut you off is still there."

As Ella turned to face the road in front of her, she saw the silver SUV. There weren't even that many cars on the road yet, and it was waiting at the traffic light about ten feet in front of them.

Ella hit the gas. "What a jerk," she sputtered under her breath. "Why put others in danger for no reason?"

She came to a screeching halt right behind the silver SUV and signaled to the driver to pull over.

"Ella, come on..." said Ricardo. "Let it go. Giving out traffic tickets is not your job."

Her jaw tightened. She knew it wasn't. "I can't let someone endanger the public."

"If Wilson finds out..."

It would be one more piece of ammunition for the captain to use against her.

She tapped on the wheel with her thumb. He was right. She should let it go. She'd disobeyed direct orders before, always for the right reasons, but the captain disagreed.

Fuck it. Whoever was in that car could have caused her to drive right into the crowd of protesters. He'd just risked the lives and well-being of several people.

She opened the door. "He won't."

Without bothering to put on her coat, she got out of the car and into the freezing air. It smelled like gas and snow, like winter, despite the leaves still on the trees and bushes.

"Hey-hey! Ho-ho! CO_2 has got to go!" yelled the crowd marching down the sidewalk to her right.

"Stop Climate Change."

"Food. For. All."

Through the yells, her short heels clunked against the asphalt as she strode to the driver's window. Even with the door closed, she could hear some sort of folk metal blasting out of the car. The man behind the wheel stared at the road in front of him like he wanted to kill it. With olive skin, long, dark-blond hair pulled up in a man bun, and a short, dark beard that wasn't much more than long stubble, he was undeniably handsome. He was dressed in a clearly expensive suit, one large, strong hand on the wheel. But a leather wristband and tattoos of some sort of Norse symbols were visible below the shirt cuff. That straight nose, the small scars on his cheek, and one across his eyebrow, plus a small birthmark by his eye—it all combined to make him look like a badass billionaire.

She put her knuckles against the window to knock when the light turned green and the car shot forward so fast she had to gasp.

"Goddamn!"

The SUV was quickly disappearing down the road between the skyscrapers. Shaking her head, she ran back to her car. She'd been talking about endangering the public, but she was the one now blocking traffic.

As she sat back in her seat, her eyes followed the silver SUV as it faded in the distance. "Got the plate number?"

Ricardo tapped his temple. "Photographic memory, remember?"

She accelerated. "Perfect. You'll need it later."

"Ella, you know you're breaking every rule Wilson set for you. Let it go."

"If you think I can let it go, clearly, you don't know me."

Letting things go had never been her strong suit. Especially things like looking for her mother, who'd walked out on her at the age of four and disappeared like she'd never existed.

Twenty-five years later, Ella was still searching.

And using police resources for personal reasons.

Which was the second reason she was on such shaky ground with Wilson. The first was insubordination. But the real problem, she'd always suspected, was that she was a woman.

Ricardo's phone rang, and he picked it up. "Sanchez. Yeah… On our way."

When he hung up, he turned to her. "Drive to the Port of Boston."

As though the silver SUV had just heard the same conversation, it turned right at the next intersection.

"What happened?" She slowed down and followed the SUV.

"Big drug bust, avocado container. Wilson is on his way there, too, and wants us on the case."

Her face fell. If Wilson was going to be there, this must be highly important.

"Okay."

"Best behavior?" said Ricardo.

She chuckled. "Do you need to remind me?"

"Obviously," he said with a smirk.

The silver SUV sped up and soon dissolved in the traffic, and Ella took a deep breath to calm down. She'd get the guy another way. Something about that face looked familiar, like she'd already seen him somewhere. She'd find out soon enough.

Fifteen minutes later, they arrived at the port area in southeast Boston. Behind the gray metal fence, large warehouses shielded a long row of blue, green, and red container cranes that darkened against the gray sky.

Ella identified herself and Ricardo at the security gate, and the guard told her to head to building A03. She passed the concrete-and-glass management building and drove between the rows of containers to the left and warehouse buildings to the right, approaching the flashing lights of police cars at the end of the straight road.

Parking the car among the other police and port police vehicles, she got out, pulling on her winter coat. Freezing sea wind blew small snowflakes that felt as sharp as needles into her face. "Give me that coffee," she said to Ricardo, who huddled into the puffy orange jacket that made him look like a basketball. His appearance often misled suspects and the public into thinking he was a goofball and, therefore, harmless. Nothing could be further from the truth. Ricardo was a better shot than Ella, and the combination of his photographic memory and sharp mind made him an excellent detective.

Someone Ella was proud to work with.

He handed it to her. "There's still a bit left."

She snatched the travel mug with a roll of her eyes. "Gee, thanks."

They walked by Wilson's gray sedan, and Ella was already mentally preparing herself. A dozen or so men and women gathered around a white container. Wilson stood out easily with his tall, heavy figure, his shoulders always slouched, his bald head under a cap. Her gaze slid over the row of cars parked on the other side of the road and she stopped, frozen.

She laid her hand on Ricardo's arm. "Is that the jerky jerk's SUV?"

He gave her a crooked smile and a chuckle. "Yup. Same plate number."

Ella growled and marched towards the group of people.

And then she saw him, how could she not—he was the tallest of them all. Even in 14 degrees Fahrenheit, he stood in his suit, coatless, as though completely unbothered by the cold.

He was talking to Wilson, who whirled around when he heard her heels clacking against the asphalt.

Along with him, the Viking god looked in her direction, and the polite expression on his face evaporated. His eyes narrowed and focused on her, looking her up and down as she walked. They were a green so dark, she could be looking at ancient moss.

Good God, he was not just looking, he was...

Devouring. Glaring. Trying to get under her skin.

Well, he wasn't doing anything for her, she decided. Didn't matter that her knees became as weak as Jell-O, or that a sudden flush of heat formed sweat droplets between her shoulder blades despite the cold, or that her cheeks felt like two furnaces.

Whoever the guy was, she wouldn't let him get away with reckless driving.

And why the hell did he look so familiar?

Wilson scowled at Ella and Ricardo. "Ah, Sanchez, O'Connor. Finally. This is Channing Hakonson—"

Ella finished, "—CEO of the Port of Boston."

The man in question held his hand out. "Pleased to meet you."

Automatically, she stretched her hand out to him and shook

his. His hand was dry and calloused, and big and hard, as though he didn't work in an office but cut wood for a living. As their hands slipped together and interconnected, a jolt of something went through her... Like a blast of fire, and was she insane, or did she glimpse golden threads that intertwined their hands?

She blinked and the image disappeared. But she didn't have time to wonder about it as something was again happening around her, just like in one of those dreams. Time stopped and slowed, and it was as though they were completely alone, he and she. Alone in the whole world. Around them, everyone froze as though on pause. And as that soft, sweet impulse of joy and heat rushed through her from his touch, she stopped breathing.

But when he removed his hand from hers, everything returned to normal. He stretched his hand out to Ricardo and shook.

Yes, Channing Hakonson.

The man who'd cost her cousin his job. The man thanks to whom she absolutely couldn't get fired now, or she'd lose the mortgage on their triple-decker in Dorchester.

Ella knew she was staring at his handsome, smug face, longing to cuff him and fine him and show him that just because he owned the largest port in the United States, that didn't mean he owned the streets of Boston or other people's lives.

But she needed to be professional for now.

She turned to Wilson. "So, what did you find?"

He gestured at a tarp covered with several rows of neatly arranged brown bags.

"Five hundred and fifty kilos. That's 1,212 pounds of cocaine."

She whistled.

"Hidden in avocado crates from Colombia. That's just one container. There may be more. There were several from Agrico Solutions—they're all being searched now."

Channing Hakonson looked at her. "I already told Mr. Wilson, if there's anything I can do, any resources you need, I'm at your disposal." Man, his voice was smooth. Low and pleasant, deep, like a rumble of thunder at the horizon, bringing relief after a long drought. He had a slight accent...that soft rolling of consonants, like he was caressing them. Something Nordic...Icelandic, perhaps...would fit the tattoos of runes and Viking patterns, that man-bun situation going on despite his suit. "Anything you need to stop the drug trafficking, you let me know."

He was saying it straight to her, and stretched out his hand with a business card between his index and middle fingers. She took it without looking, struggling to stop herself from tearing it into pieces. She wanted nothing to do with the arrogant jerk.

She opened her mouth to say something, but his phone rang and he answered it, raising one finger to her, in a "hold that thought" gesture.

"Coming." He hung up. "I apologize, I need to leave. But, Detectives and Captain Wilson, I'm serious. Anything you need, just let me know. I'm leaving you in the hands of Peter van Beek, the port manager."

The man in question nodded to her, his deeply set, dark eyes reminded her of a mouse's. He looked like a guy who worked in a cubicle all his life—clean haircut, blue dress shirt, woolen business coat. and a small belly, the inevitable result of a sedentary lifestyle.

"Anything you need," said van Beek.

Ella nodded, her eyes glued to Channing Hakonson as he marched towards his car. His stride was long, and there was something of a predator—a wolf on a hunt—in the movement of his broad shoulders and long, muscular legs, apparent even under the slacks of his charcoal gray suit.

She shook her head. "The drugs. Any ideas? Did the FBI tell you anything?"

Wilson sighed and rubbed his chin. "Actually, they did." He gave Ella a long stare. "I was mulling over if I'm making the right decision giving the case to you, O'Connor."

Ella bit her lower lip to stop herself from defending her actions. She knew she wasn't supposed to look up the license plate numbers for her private purposes, but finding her mom was more important than any risk to her job.

And she had no regrets about refusing to arrest peaceful protesters camping in City Hall Square. She'd disobey orders again if she had to. Someone needed to do something about climate change and the subsequent food shortage.

"This is your final chance to prove yourself, O'Connor," Wilson said. "I already have enough to get you fired. But I've been holding off out of respect for your father. Strike three, and you're out."

The mortgage, she reminded herself. Her dad in a wheel-chair. Her brother with special needs. Her aunt and uncle. Her cousin Rob with a wife and a baby on the way. They all depended on her salary and ability to pay the mortgage. What would she do if she lost this job?

"Yes, sir," she said.

"Good." Wilson smirked, his fat lips lifting on one side. How he always smelled like barbecue, Ella had no idea. "The FBI got a tip from an informant in the Dominican street gangs that a powerful figure in the Port of Boston covers large drug-trafficking operations. That's why ever since Channing Hakonson became the owner and the CEO of the port, they've had almost no drug busts. Because, guess who that powerful figure is?"

A car revved, and the three of them watched the silver SUV speed down the street like a rocket.

Wilson met her eyes, his steely gray gaze cold and impassive.

"Prove your worth. Find proof against him, or you're fired."

TWO

The gods were playing with him.

How could the police have found cocaine on the same day his two scientists had made a breakthrough?

As Channing drove, he glanced in the mirror at the flashing lights of the police cars. Detective Ella O'Connor stood there, staring after him.

And what were the chances that today he'd meet this woman?

With icy-blue eyes, the posture of a Valkyrie, and the body of Freya, the goddess of love. With long, blond hair he ached to tangle his fingers in, high cheekbones, full, kissable lips, and porcelain skin, she reminded him of the Nordic beauties he'd seen so much of growing up. And yet he couldn't remember meeting a more striking woman. The gray pantsuit didn't do her athletic figure justice, although she'd look good wearing a burlap sack.

When her eyes had locked with his, it felt as if Thor had thrown a lightning bolt right into his chest. Something about her looked familiar, like he'd seen eyes like those before, although he had no recollection of when or how.

In the mirror, her figure disappeared into the distance as he drove through the heart of the port. Mountains of coal and ore, walls of containers, and warehouse buildings flashed by. To his right, cranes lifted containers from the dock, stacking them in multicolored layers on the waiting ships.

Beyond them, across the silver blue of Boston Bay, across the vastness of the Atlantic Ocean, laid his home.

Norway. Only not the Norway of the twenty-first century.

For fourteen years, he'd been waiting to leave this time. He hadn't engaged in any relationships, hadn't tied himself to anyone.

There were no true gods here. No glory. No honor.

Money was god. And the powerful people in this time worshipped at its altar with their fancy cars, mansions, and private jets. Even the poor begged for blessings they seldom saw.

Money had come easily to him. And the old gods were probably laughing, highly entertained by his life.

Well, perhaps not the gods, but the Norns. Those three ladies as old as time, and as powerful. They were the ones who defined the destiny of men and gods.

One of them had sent him here, on that damned day in the ninth century when King Harald had suddenly wanted to kill him. They must be laughing at his attempts to return, to take control of his own destiny. But they would soon see the power that money could bring.

His gaze returned to the sky over the vast ocean. Something was brewing out there, in those heavy clouds out on the horizon carrying snowstorms and ice. This sudden Nordic weather, the huge drug bust, and meeting that woman—it all set the hairs on the back of his neck on end. The feeling was cold, and dark, and urged his hand to grab his sword.

Shaking the heavy, sucking longing off, Channing parked his car before a simple warehouse building that didn't distinguish itself from the row of other warehouses lining the middle of the port. Building M05 was the size of half a football stadium. The three-story concrete walls didn't have any windows but two gates, large enough for the freight crane to pass through, not to mention the trucks with containers.

Channing's throat clenched against the stabbing wind shoving gusts into his face as he strode from the car to the entrance.

Inside the warehouse wasn't any warmer. Crates of goods, cardboard boxes with metal parts, screws, drills, and tools were stacked on top of one another. Next to the empty, rusty crane cabin stood a forklift. Chains hung from the ceiling. It smelled like dust, old machine oil, and metal.

No one had been here for years, except Channing and the two people who waited for him underground.

Making his way through the maze of shelves and crates, he turned left and then right and left again. He approached the pile of boxes by the wall where, hidden behind a regular electric switch, was a code panel.

Channing punched the code in, then the row of boxes that he stood next to moved to the right.

A square opening was revealed in the floor, and a simple metal staircase illuminated by yellow lights led underground. He turned around and scanned the dark warehouse. Wind wailed in gaps under the gates and the entrance door, but there was no other sound. Throwing a last glance around, he descended the stairs. He pressed a button on the wall, and the trap door closed over his head.

The basement was two stories down. In the middle of the room, elevated on a solid, steel construction, was a giant golden spindle. Norse runes and curly Viking patterns were engraved on its surface.

Long tables lined the walls of the lab with equipment, some of which hadn't been acquired legally. The basement itself didn't exist in the official port plans. There was always a faint chemical scent here—something clean, like whiteboard marker and bleach.

By the farther wall, half of which was a giant whiteboard covered with formulas, drawings, charts, and equations, were two figures in blue lab coats. They were engaged in a loud discussion about one of the formulas. As Channing continued down the stairs, the clang of his shoes against the metal echoed off the walls, but the scientists didn't pay him any attention.

The woman, Dr. Georgina Brandon, a short, thin Black woman in her early thirties, rubbed her finger against her chin, her other hand propped against her waist. "So it is like a Tipler Cylinder, only it won't need to be infinite or ten times denser than the sun's mass."

Munchie, or Dr. Miles Mochizuki, a tall Japanese American man, chewed thoughtfully on a granola bar. "Um...yeah, but we still need to get a few billion revolutions per minute."

"According to this, we can." She looked at him, tapping a whiteboard marker against her lower lip. "Or are we missing something?"

Channing stood behind them, staring at the formula they'd been discussing. Not that he understood the theory of general or special relativity, or cosmic strings, but what he could see was a large formula written in blue marker in what Channing had learned over the past seven years was Munchie's curly, even handwriting. Only, one $/w(i)$ at the end of the equation was written in red marker and in what looked like different handwriting.

Channing said, "Is that the breakthrough?"

They both glanced at him over their shoulders and said, "Yes."

"Great. What does it tell us?"

Georgina walked to the whiteboard and uncapped the marker. "Well." She began writing a calculation mirroring the formula. "It tells us that you were absolutely right about the shape of the spindle that we needed for the time machine." Her hand kept moving, producing curly letters upon letters like lace. "It tells us that the spindle, upon achieving three billion rotations per minute, creates the CTCs—the closed timelike curves—around itself. And as it achieves that speed, any further spin takes one about one second back or forward in time, depending on the direction of the rotation. That speed also creates a vacuum and works with gravity pulses as opposed to fighting them."

Channing scratched his chin. "Right. Didn't you know all that already?"

Munchie took another bite of the granola bar and said through a mouthful, "Yeah. But what we didn't know was how to achieve the speed of rotation that would be equal to or greater than the speed of light."

Hope expanded in Channing's chest like a hot-air balloon. "And now you do?"

Georgina wrote, *1,000 megawatts*. "We do." She looked back at him. "This much."

"I have no idea what that number represents."

"It's enough power to meet the needs of a city the size of Boston."

Channing's stomach dropped. "Odin's ass... Is this even

possible? You said we may not have the technology to travel in time in our generation. How did you even get to this?"

Munchie and Georgina exchanged a glance. Georgina crossed her arms over her chest. "It was Munchie."

"It wasn't me."

"Not that you know of," said Georgina.

Munchie crumpled the granola bar wrapping and threw it into a wastepaper basket, missing it. "It wasn't me."

"So if it wasn't you and it wasn't Georgina..." Channing's skin prickled. "Then who? Did you let anyone in? You know you're legally not allowed to say a word to anyone."

Georgina sighed. "We didn't say a word. Seven years, Mr. Hakonson."

Munchie took out another granola bar and broke the wrapping. "We came in this morning, and it was just there."

Channing tapped one finger against the surface of the table.

"How could it just be there?"

"I have an idea," Munchie said, taking the first bite. "If we're trying to make time travel work, and we know the technology may not exist in our generation, then who's not to say that someone from the future, when the technology does exist, didn't come and give us a clue."

Georgina snorted, but Channing wasn't laughing. He'd never told the two why he'd insisted on the shape of the spindle for the time machine. And he'd never told a soul why he was so interested in time travel. Not the real reason, anyway.

As far as the two scientists were concerned, he was a sort of Elon Musk type with a scientific interest and a ton of money to burn.

They had no idea how true Munchie's crazy idea could be.

Channing's jaw muscles worked. "Can this be done?"

Munchie blinked at the number as he kept chewing. "That depends, boss. Can you get a generation seven modular nuclear reactor?"

Munchie looked at Channing through his rimless glasses, dark eyes unsmiling.

"Are you serious?" Channing leaned on the edge of a table. "A nuclear goddamn reactor?"

"Seventh generation," said Georgina. "They're not even officially invented yet."

Channing shoved both hands through his hair, stopping before his bun. "What are you saying?"

Georgina shrugged. "Generation five was approved by the International Atomic Energy Agency last year. Generation six is being tested in different countries officially. Generation seven... Officially, there are only theories on how to make it safer and more powerful than the previous versions. Most importantly, it can power on quickly, almost like a household device, whereas the previous generations need days until they're operation ready. Based on rumors, the Russians managed to create an antimatter and seventh-generation reactor, and energy levels are close to those produced by the sun."

Channing cocked his head. "What does it all mean for our project?"

"To travel in time, boss, you need a sun to power your spindle. So if you don't want to go into space and take your spindle with you, you need to bring one of those generation seven reactors here. If the mountain won't come to Muhammad, and such."

Channing's hand curled around the edge of the table.

"A freaking nuclear reactor..." he whispered.

His mind raced, considering different scenarios.

"Let me guess," Channing said. "It's not strictly legal to own one."

Georgina went to the giant spindle and put her hand on the smooth surface.

"The Nuclear Regulatory Commission controls the radioactive materials that nuclear reactors use. Reactors need to be approved by the commission and go through a series of permitting processes. I'm guessing that takes months, maybe years. And then you would need to explain why you need the reactor, which, obviously, is out of the question." She gestured around the lab.

"I don't have a year. We've been working on this for seven years already."

He walked to the stairs.

"Find another way," he threw over his shoulder.

Munchie swallowed his food. "There's no other way, dude."

Channing massaged his face with one hand. "Odin's feet, isn't a nuclear reactor extremely dangerous?"

Georgina exchanged a glance with Munchie, whose smirk fell.

"It is."

Channing closed his eyes briefly, clenching his teeth. "Isn't it easier to move the machine somewhere where it can be powered up?"

Georgina looked the spindle up and down. "Name one nuclear plant director that would agree to this."

Channing growled as he turned and started ascending the stairs. "Where's the fucking Norn when I need her," he said.

"What?" Munchie said.

"Nothing," Channing said. "It will be done."

Yes, it would be done. Because he was a man who got things done. Impossible things. Crazy things. He was a man conceived in the twenty-first century, born in the ninth, and thrown back into the twenty-first when he was eighteen.

He was a man who'd risen from nothing to owner and CEO.

He was a man who'd go back home no matter what the Norns had planned for him.

He was a man who defied destiny.

THREE

"Can you deliver it or not?" Channing asked into his burner phone as he walked out of building Mo5.

He had several burner phones in the lab for situations like this. It wasn't the first time he'd had to obtain something that was hard to find for the time machine. There didn't seem to be anything he couldn't get...for a price.

The voice on the other end of the line was distorted. "A seventh-generation nuclear reactor? Ha! I can't."

Damn it. Channing closed the door behind him and turned the key. "Do you know someone?"

As silence hung on the phone, Channing walked towards his car. He realized the snowfall had died down, but the wind had picked up.

The person sighed. "I might." The line went dead.

Well, that was the best he could hope for right now. As he walked to his car, his hands itched for his sword, craving physical activity to release the tension accumulating in his shoulders. He hadn't stopped training on his sword since he'd arrived here fourteen years ago.

Even though he'd never use the sword to fight in this century, it kept him in excellent shape. And ready to fight when he returned to the Viking Age.

He unlocked the door of his car, but just as he was about to get in, a movement near the far corner of the M05 building caught his eye. Something gray and brown...

He froze, one foot in the car, his hand on the door.

A wolf was sitting by the corner of the building, panting like a dog and staring straight at him.

A wolf?

Channing blinked. He'd never seen one in the twenty-first century. The closest wolf to here was surely in a zoo. Was it, maybe, a dog? No, Channing knew the features of wolves very well—he'd had to protect himself against them several times back in the ninth century.

Seeing one in the middle of a seaport in the city of Boston was as bizarre as it would be to see a real Viking. Yes, this was a wolf, but it must be domesticated, why else would it watch Channing so calmly...

Almost friendly.

And then, his eyes focused on something else he hadn't noticed before.

A white Ford Taurus.

Inside, Ella O'Connor and Ricardo Sanchez sat staring right at him. He sputtered an oath. They must have followed him, must have seen him go into the building and come out.

What a fucking day.

He took his foot back out, closed the door, and walked towards the Taurus. As he approached, Ella rolled down her window and smiled at him angelically.

Channing put his hand on the roof and leaned down to be on the same eye level. "Detectives."

Ella cocked her head, her brilliant blue eyes flashing. "Mr. Hakonson," she said with an exaggerated sweetness. "Can we talk?"

The dark eyes of Ricardo Sanchez were hard on him.

Channing nodded. "Perhaps, in my office—"

"What's in that building?" Ella interrupted, the fake smile still on her face.

"Just follow me to my office." Without waiting for a response, he turned away and walked to his car.

As he started the engine, he threw a glance at the corner of M05. The wolf was gone.

When he'd parked in the lot of the main office building, he didn't look back at the detectives who followed him. They hadn't come for small talk, and he wasn't in the mood for chitchat.

When they arrived at the sixth floor, where his office was, his secretary, Shelly, stood and said her usual, "Good morning, Mr. Hakonson!"

He stopped before Shelly, who observed the two detectives from behind her librarian-style glasses.

He leaned forward. "Good morning. Cancel my meetings this morning. I'll be in with the detectives."

"Of course, sir." She looked at Ella and Ricardo. "Can I get you some coffee? Tea?"

"Nothing for me," said Ella.

As Ricardo opened his mouth, his phone rang. "Sanchez... Yeah." He frowned and met Ella's eyes. "They located the captain of the *Pijao*. He was sightseeing. They have him at the station for questioning."

Ella looked at Channing with those sharp eyes that seemed to pierce him like two scramasaxes. "You go. I'll have a chat with Mr. Hakonson and then join you."

"Sure. I'll get a ride with Wilson."

When Ricardo left, Channing gestured towards his office door, his stomach suddenly light at the thought of being alone with the beautiful detective. As she walked past him, he looked her up and down and wished he hadn't because another onrush of blood flowed to his already woken cock. Her hourglass figure moved deliciously under the cheap suit that attempted to hide all her best parts.

He reached from behind her and opened the glass door, allowing her to pass through.

Her back as straight as a pole, her round ass swaying seductively, she walked into his office in front of him. She looked around the large space. He had it decorated in a sleek, simple contemporary style, high-end enough to communicate he was successful. Those were the rules of the game, not that he cared about the cost.

A large desk made of grayish-white driftwood faced the door. Two walls were floor-to-ceiling windows overlooking the port, Reserved Channel and Logan Airport on the other side of Boston Main Channel. A piece of modern art—wood and chrome waves interweaving, playing together—hung above a white leather couch. A massive table for meetings occupied the other side of the room.

"So," he said as he sat down in an armchair next to the couch. "Tell me."

She contemplated him for a moment, then came towards the chair opposite his but didn't take a seat. Instead, she crossed her arms over her chest. "You tell me, Mr. Hakonson. While you were doing whatever you were doing in that warehouse you went to so abruptly, we did a background check on you."

He tapped his thumb against the leather arm of the chair. "Is that so?"

"Mmm." She walked closer to the waves. "There's no one

quite like you, is there? Your mother died when you were eighteen. No father indicated on your birth certificate."

At the mention of his mother, he tensed. That was the official story he'd had someone on the dark web create for him.

His real mother was an American. She'd gotten pregnant with Channing by her boyfriend, a Mafia boss named Dan Esposito. He was an abusive motherfucker, and she'd basically run away from the year 2019 to the Viking Age.

Ella O'Connor kept talking. "You started working in the Port of Boston at the age of nineteen. Buying and flipping property on the side. A couple of lucky investments allowed you to gather quite a bit of capital in only a few short years."

When he'd first arrived, he'd gone to Norway, to the rune stone in Lomdalen, trying to get back to his own time. But nothing had worked. So he'd returned to Boston, where his mother was from, and to what he knew...ships. Trade.

At the same time, he'd kept searching for an answer—how could he get back? He'd begun devouring Icelandic sagas about Vikings and Norse mythology. One of them told a story of Jarl Hakon of Lomdalen, whose son disappeared into thin air. Two years later, his wife, daughter, and younger son died when an enemy locked them in their great hall and burned it to the ground.

Knowing this, Channing had to find a way to go back and save them.

That was why he'd become rich. That was why he'd come to own the port. To make enough money to hire scientists and build a time machine, and to have a place where he could do so undetected. With science on his side, he didn't need Norns. Using a machine, he could travel to whatever time he chose.

Channing tapped on the side of his chair again. "I don't believe in luck."

She met his gaze, her blue eyes steely. "Neither do I.

Therefore, one might wonder how someone with no education, no money, and no connections became one of the most influential people in Boston."

"This is America. Isn't achieving success through hard work the dream all you Americans strive for?"

As the words left his mouth, he knew he'd made a mistake. And she caught it. "You Americans? Aren't *you* an American also? That's what your birth certificate says."

Goddamn it. "I am."

"Then what about your accent?"

He was tired of lying. That was what he'd been doing for fourteen years. Pretending to be someone he wasn't. That was why he never became close to anyone. Had no friends. No woman.

No one.

"It's Icelandic. I've spent many summers in Iceland."

Old Norse, the tongue Vikings spoke in the ninth century, was a dead language, and its closest equivalent was modern Icelandic.

"Hmm. Gossip columnists love stories about you. A mysterious, sword-fighting, Old Norse-teaching billionaire who collects Viking artifacts and sponsors Viking events in Maine."

Or a lonely man, desperate to find a connection to his roots.

"What do my personal interests have to do with the drugs, Detective?"

She shrugged. "Perhaps nothing. Or everything. There are a few things about you that don't add up. I still don't understand how you managed to take the Port of Boston from bankrupt to the largest port in the United States in just seven years."

"I bought it using angel investors, and I knew right away where the weaknesses were since I had worked here repairing and maintaining ships. I've always had an affinity for ships and trade. I don't see why my hard work and passion for what I do has suddenly become reason for suspicion."

She gave him a hard look. "Very simple. A container of drugs was found in your port."

He chuckled, though uneasiness scraped at his gut. There was something threatening in her stiff posture, her penetrating, icy stare.

He leaned back. "Drugs are often smuggled through ports. We do our best, but it's impossible to catch them all. We don't have the means to scan every container, and exotic fruit containers are always on a deadline. It's a weak point of every seaport and every customs."

As she ran a hand along the driftwood surface of his desk, he couldn't help imagining those slim fingers trailing down his bare torso, followed by her full lips. "All true," she said. "And you've done a splendid job of reducing the amount of cocaine found at your port since you took over."

The heaviness tightened in his stomach, and he put one ankle on his knee. "Yes."

If she was digging, he wasn't going to make it any easier for her. This was like any negotiation, like any power struggle. His father had taught him this. *The one who can keep the silence wins.*

So he kept silent and just stared at her pretty profile. He wondered if her beauty served her well or failed her in her job.

It was certainly distracting for him.

She turned to him. "And yet you became a billionaire in a few short years. A self-made man. From nobody to one of the one-percenters."

He kept staring at her. "If you have a question, Detective, do not hesitate to ask it before another century passes by."

She raised one eyebrow, clearly unimpressed. "One may

wonder if your quick riches and the low rate of cocaine seizures at your port may be connected."

Channing set both feet on the ground and leaned forward, elbows braced on his knees. "Do you seriously suspect me of smuggling drugs?"

Her expression hardened, icy-blue eyes darkening like a winter storm.

Like the eyes of a she-wolf on a hunt.

"What is in building M05?" she asked.

He was on his feet and stood before her. He grabbed her by her upper arm, pulling her closer. Her scent filled his nostrils, citrusy and surprisingly deep. It was a mixture of some perfume she wore and her own scent, and the combination made his heart drum like a fist in his chest.

Her cheeks flushed, her pupils dilated, and her sweet, plump lips parted. Her body was pleasant against him, soft electricity charging through him where he was holding her arm and against his torso where her breasts were touching him.

He inhaled and regretted it right away. Her scent made him want to bury his face in her hair and breathe it in like a drug. "Why do you think there's anything suspicious about building M05, Detective?"

She jerked her arm, trying to free herself from his grip, but he couldn't let her go. "Answer me if you have nothing to hide."

He heard her, but her words didn't register in his mind. He wanted her. He didn't know her. He'd talked to her for only a few minutes. But he'd wanted her from the moment he'd seen her back at the container.

From where he came from, there weren't so many restrictions and social niceties as today. If he wanted a woman, and if she was willing, he took her.

And he wanted her. The Viking in him roared and thumped his ax against his shield, ready to take what was his.

And he did.

He wrapped his other arm around her waist and leaned down to claim her mouth—

Sharp pain shot through his foot as she stomped on his shoe. With a suppressed groan, he relaxed his grip for a moment, and she slithered out of his embrace and twisted his arm so that it straightened into a single line. With one good punch from her other hand, she could break his arm.

"Sexual harassment is a punishable offense, Mr. Hakonson," she said through her teeth. "So be especially careful with female officers of the law. Unlike a lot of women who are intimidated by assholes like you, we are not."

He was like lava, boiling with anger, desire, and admiration. Who was this sweet Valkyrie? She had teeth and claws and could give as much as he gave. Their eyes were locked in a silent fight, but beneath the hardness of her blue stare was fire, too. She may be pretending that he didn't affect her, but she wanted him.

His phone rang.

"Do you mind?" he said softly, unable to turn away from her pretty face. "Or are you going to hold my arm all day long?"

She let go and stepped back, breathing heavily, but visibly trying to calm herself down.

"Hakonson," he said into his phone.

"Mr. Hakonson," said a male voice that sounded vaguely familiar. "Word is you are looking for something I can deliver."

Forgetting the beautiful detective, Channing turned his back to her and walked to the window, his gut churning.

"Who is this?" he said.

He could feel the detective's stare burning two holes into his back.

"Leo Esposito," the voice said. "You might have heard of me."

A cold snake coiled in Channing's gut. Oh yes, he'd heard of Leonardo Esposito all right.

Most people in New England had. He was the head of the Esposito Mafia, wanted by both the police and the FBI.

But what no one knew, including Leo himself, was that he was Channing's biological grandfather.

FOUR

"Everything all right?" Dad asked as he rolled into Ella's room in his wheelchair.

She looked up from the folder containing Channing's file. She was sitting on her bed, the table lamp casting light on the photo of the handsome man she'd questioned earlier that day.

"Sure, Dad." She set the file aside.

Ted, her half brother, was long asleep and Gloria, her stepmom, must be in bed with a book.

Dad stopped his wheelchair by her side. He still had the look of a cop who assumed everyone was hiding something. "Saw the light under your door. Thought maybe something was on your mind."

She chuckled. "I'm not a teenager anymore, Dad."

He smiled. "Sadly, you're not." His gaze dropped to the file. "Is that the new case?"

She pursed her lips. "Yeah. I'm just looking for clues... The main suspect's life pretty much doesn't exist until the age of eighteen."

Bryan chuckled into his moustache and looked at his hands. "I knew a person like that once."

She frowned. "Who?"

He cleared his throat and looked straight at her with a hint of sadness behind his eyes. "Your mom."

Your mom... The two words that could knock air out of her lungs like nothing else. Even after twenty-five years.

"Yeah...tell me about it. I know she was Norwegian or something, right? I've looked through everything I could find in the police records."

"Is that how you got caught?"

She nodded sadly. "I know I shouldn't have used the police database for private reasons. But it was worth it to me."

"You know what she'd say about it?"

Ella chuckled. "Something about destiny..."

"Yeah. I met her when we were both very young, and yet sometimes she sounded like an old lady. Especially with her accent."

"She had an accent?" It was odd that Ella didn't know that. It was funny how memory worked. She didn't remember an accent, but she couldn't forget those piercing blue eyes, same as hers.

"A very soft one. She was here on vacation from Norway she said, an escape from her family. We fell in love so quickly, and she just never wanted to go back."

They weren't married, otherwise Ella would have had a legal document about her mom, which would help. But there was no paper trail. No airplane ticket, no passport, nothing.

All that was left of her was an embroidery and a photo of her with Ella.

"Did you have any signs?" Ella stood up and walked to her dresser. She opened a drawer, took out a shoebox, and retrieved the photo and the embroidery. "That she'd leave?"

In the photo, a young, pretty woman with blond hair and blue eyes, wearing a green sundress, gave two-year-old Ella a kiss on the cheek.

Pain pierced Ella in the chest as she gently wiped the glass of the frame.

Dad sighed. "Not sure. I started talking about getting married, and maybe that was when I started seeing that fear in her eyes. She was blabbering more about destiny and such… She started having insomnia, would go for a week without leaving the house. So I suppose those were signs of something. I never thought they were signs that she'd leave." He met her eyes. "She loved you, hon."

Ella's vision blurred, and she wiped the tears with the back of her sleeve. "I begged her to stay. How can a mother leave a begging child forever?"

Ella retrieved the third thing that was left of Mom from the shoebox.

Her goodbye note.

Ella opened the folded paper and read the script written in capital letters, almost like that of a child. Almost like her mother hadn't had a lot of practice writing.

I AM SORRY. IT HAS TO BE.

Ella chuckled and laid the note back into the shoebox. Mom had probably meant to make her feel better with the note, but all it had done was stab her in the gut.

Seven words. That was all she deserved? Four years and seven words?

"She could be dead," said Bryan.

Ella sat back on her bed and placed the folded embroidery on her lap. "No. I saw her. Two years ago. I saw her in the city. She was getting into that car, you remember, which is why I looked up that plate number."

Bryan nodded. "You were four when she left, and this is the

only picture we have of her. You may not recognize her after twenty-five years. You probably confused her with someone else."

She knew this might be true, but something within her said it had been her mother.

And then she'd had that dream, one of *those* dreams. Where she relived an event and could change it.

The dreams always had this strange blurriness, the sounds and voices were echoey, and things moved as slow or as fast as she wanted them to.

In the dream, it was a sunny summer day, and Ella was standing at the entrance of Columbus Park, chatting with Ricardo. They were getting coffee after interviewing a suspect on a case.

There was a flash of green in her side vision, and when she looked, a woman in her sixties wearing a long sundress, just like in the photo, walked towards a car parked where it wasn't supposed to be. Her blond hair was done in a braid like a crown around her head. She had something that glistened like gold in her hand—a purse perhaps. She got into a black car where Ella had thought she noticed two more blond heads. And then the car drove off.

That was exactly what had happened.

Only, in her dream, Ella had paused the moment right before the woman got into the car and yelled, "Mom!"

The woman froze, looked up, and her icy-blue eyes met Ella's. Recognition flashed across her face in an almost unnoticeable microexpression. And then she got into the car and it drove away.

In the dream, Ella had sharpened the focus, returned the speed to normal, and removed the echoey sounds. She'd woven this event into the material of reality.

Or at least, she'd convinced herself that it had become real, that she had somehow changed the original event to match her dream.

She'd always woken up confused after those dreams, uncertain what was real and what was her mind's fantasy. The rational woman in her told her she simply had a vivid imagination and the emotional trauma of an abandoned child. Those factors combined made her want to believe this was real.

But the plate number from her dream had led to a stolen car in Denver. And the second time she had run the license plate a few months ago, which was when Wilson had caught her, she discovered that the car had been found abandoned in 2019 in central Boston, a week after her dream.

Ella knew she hadn't mistaken the woman for someone else, but she didn't want to tell her dad about her weird dreams. "Who knows," she replied.

She unfolded the embroidery. A scene from Norse mythology played out before her eyes. Wolves were eating a human corpse. A man in a medieval tunic and pants and a woman in a Norse apron-dress had knives deep in each other's chests. Three roosters—one crimson, one golden, and one dark red—sat on a large tree with their beaks open, probably crowing. Snow blanketed everything, and a black sun was in the sky. Volcanoes were erupting in the distance and a wall of fire was coming into the picture from the side. The god Thor had his hammer Mjölnir high above his head as he was about to fight a giant snake, who, as Ella had learned, was the world serpent Jörmungandr.

"You know what that is?" Dad asked.

Ella fingered the edge of the thick, sturdy fabric. "Ragnarök, the end of the world from Norse mythology."

"She liked that kind of stuff," Dad said. "Liked to embroider Viking scenes—a man and a woman coming together, getting married. Happy things. The end of the world...that was an unusual theme for her, I have to say."

"I wonder why she left that one," Ella said.

And as she studied the wolves and the snow and the roosters, she wondered if it was symbolic because twenty-five years ago, Mom's disappearance ended Ella's happy little childhood world and left her heart in an eternal winter.

FIVE

As Channing ran, the back of his neck prickled with the sense of danger. He felt exposed, watched, like prey under the eyes of an invisible hunter.

He sped up, the asphalt of the pier flashing under his shoes as he jogged through Christopher Columbus Waterfront Park. The dawn had just begun to lighten the sky, the air crisp and as sharp as the blade of a new scramasax.

His heart drummed, his muscles singing with the pleasure of movement. Unlike those who had been born in this time, he didn't listen to music during his morning jogs, which allowed him to listen for signs of danger. But nothing was out of the ordinary in the water splashing against the pier and the boats, the pounding of his shoes against the asphalt, the distant hum of cars, and the wind blowing in his ears.

There was no one on the benches, no one on the dark grass. A female jogger in a baseball hat ran towards him. His mood lifted for a split second as he thought it might be Detective O'Connor, but the woman passed him by, giving him a lingering look. It wasn't Ella.

Ella...

As he scanned the park to his right, looking for movement in the shadows, he thought of her intelligent gaze, the sweet, full mouth, the curve of her seductive behind.

Yesterday morning when his grandfather had called, he'd seen in her eyes that she knew he was up to something. She knew the call was something he didn't want her to hear.

Shelly had come in saying that he was already late for his meeting with the financial department and saved him from having to ask Ella to leave, which would have raised her suspicions even more. They'd agreed to meet later today, after which she'd left the room without a word.

His longing for her was seriously inconvenient. Fucking a police detective who was investigating drug smuggling in his port was a terrible idea.

But he'd never wanted anyone like he wanted her.

It didn't need to be emotional; it didn't need to be anything serious. Purely physical. Lust. Get it out of his system and move on with the damned time machine.

The question he'd asked his black market guy had been answered faster than he'd thought.

And the answer was in the hands of his grandfather. The thought of Leonardo Esposito made his gut churn. He'd sworn never to have anything to do with the man, even though he was the only blood relative Channing had in this century.

But, he supposed, destiny had other plans.

Channing was approaching the end of the park and was turning left, about to jog along the red brick Waterline Hotel, when the screeching of car tires made his pulse jump.

Right in the middle of the pedestrian zone, a black SUV sped towards him.

The prickling at the back of his neck turned into a burning. To surprise the driver, he veered in a different direction and ran

as fast as he could. Arms and legs pumping, he gave it everything he had. His breath rushed in and out rhythmically, his
lungs aching. The car roared behind him.

Faster. Faster!

Something shiny and black flashed to his left and stopped
before him, blocking the way. Two men in dark suits spilled out
of the car. Where was a sword or even a kitchen knife when he
needed one? He turned yet again, but arms wrapped around his
shoulders from behind.

The Viking within him growled like a wolf, jubilant.

A real fight, a fight for his life. He hadn't had one in fourteen years. That was what he knew how to do, what his father
had trained him for—protecting his life and his family.

He shoved his elbow into the man's solar plexus. The man
grunted but didn't let him go.

He was about to drive his elbow into the man's stomach
again when the other guy appeared in front of him and hit him
in the jaw. Channing's skull exploded in pain as his head
snapped backwards. A blow to his cheekbone made his ears
ring.

Fighting his disorientation and clinging to the battle rage,
he grabbed the arms of the bastard who held him. He had
fought countless battles in the ninth century, and how he
missed it.

Someone pressed a cloth to his nose and his mouth. A
sharp, chemical smell hit his nostrils. He clutched at the hand,
moaning, fighting to peel it off his face.

They weren't giving him a chance to fight like a man.

Darkness took him.

He woke up to the feeling of movement and the lulling
sound of a car engine. Light came from the windows of the
car, but his vision was still too blurry to distinguish where
he was going. Then the cloth with the chemical scent

pressed to his face again and once again he sank into oblivion.

Light stung his eyes, and he jerked upright, slowly coming back to his senses. He was sitting on a couch in a room with grand, mullioned windows and a long balcony overlooking the ocean. Marbled beige-brown wallpaper covered the walls. The dark wood furniture was elegant and European. Four marble columns supported the ceiling. Paintings of the faces of Italian sculptures hung on the walls. There was a round bar on the other side of the room, and a guy in a dark suit was shaking a cocktail mixer, glaring at Channing in a silent warning.

By the window, an old man with a long ponytail painted a seashore landscape.

Distantly, Channing remarked to himself that the painting wasn't bad.

No.

He couldn't care less if Leonardo Esposito was the most talented painter in the world.

He had raised the rapist who had fathered Channing.

Channing wondered every day why the Norn had chosen to send him into 2007, twelve years before his conception.

Why he'd had to live in the same city as his father, a Mafia boss, and his mother, a medical student, who had no idea their grown son was walking the same streets, breathing the same air, and even watching them from a distance.

The hardest part had been to live in the same city as Dan Esposito and not kill him or report him to the police. To wait for him to meet Mom, to seduce her, and to continuously rape her and abuse her.

And Channing had had to stand by doing nothing so that he wouldn't prevent his own birth—but, most importantly, the births of his sister and brother.

Probably, the Norn had simply wanted to torture him.

At least the bastard was dead now.

Channing rose to his feet, his head still spinning.

"What the fuck, Leonardo?" he said.

The guy by the bar put his mixer down, his hand moving casually to his waist, where, Channing guessed, he must keep his gun.

Leonardo looked at him over his shoulder, dark eyes sharp. "Ah. You're awake."

Returning to his canvas, he made several strokes of white paint, and they started to look like sails in the middle of the ocean.

Leonardo scooped a bit of paint onto his brush from his palette. "There's water on the coffee table. You'll feel better if you drink. Forgive the harsh treatment. Had to be done. You can't know where you are."

How much time passed since the kidnapping? The antique clock showed 9:15 a.m.

He was missing his appointment with Ella.

He stood up and walked through the large space between the couch and the coffee table. "Where's my phone?"

The thug came out from behind the bar, his hand now visibly on the gun strapped to his belt.

Leonardo leaned closer to the painting and made two strokes. A seagull. "Leave him, Joe. Channing, your phone will be returned to you when you're back in Boston. Want a drink?"

Channing shook his head once, fuming. Kidnapping him for a peaceful sit-down, taking his phone away, and then offering him drinks? The fucker wanted to show him he had all the power and control.

The only thing he could do was play along for now. "Sure."

With a heavy glance at him, Joe returned to stand behind the bar. When Channing sat on the barstool, the man poured a drink into two martini glasses, put one in front of Channing and took the other one to Leonardo. He put the brush down, wiped his hands with a cloth, and took the glass.

"*Grazie*," he said.

Leonardo came to stand next to Channing. He must be in his late sixties, but he was still a tall and imposing man. Had Channing inherited his height from his father's side?

His dark eyes fell on Channing and bored into him, sharp and shiny as a weasel's. "You know, Mr. Hakonson, ever since I first saw your picture—it was in an article about you buying the port, I think—it struck me how much you remind me of my son, Daniel."

Channing didn't want to remind anyone of a rapist and a criminal.

"You don't happen to have Italian blood, do you?" Leonardo asked.

Channing's jaw ticked. "I am of Norse descent," he said, even though it was untrue.

But he had been raised a Viking. And that was who he would always be. No matter whose seed had contributed to his existence.

"Yes, well..." Leonardo raised his glass. "*Salute.*"

Channing raised his glass without great desire to do so and emptied the contents into his throat. He glanced at Joe with a chuckle.

"A bodyguard and a bartender. Not just a pretty face, hey?" Joe scowled at him.

Leonardo smacked his lips. "You like Joe's martini? Wait until you try this."

Walking behind the bar, Leonardo started pouring gin and vermouth without measuring. He added a handful of ice cubes and squeezed a half lemon above the tumbler.

Shaking it vigorously, he glanced at Channing. "So. You need a nuclear reactor."

Channing's jaw tightened.

"I didn't expect to get it from you," he said.

Leonardo opened the mixer and poured the cocktails into two glasses. "Why do you need it?"

"None of your business."

Leonardo opened a jar of olives and put three on a cocktail stick. "Tell me one thing. Should I move my operations away from Boston?"

"I don't know. Should you?"

"It depends. Is it about to become a nuclear wasteland?"

He plunged the cocktail stick with olives into Channing's martini and shifted the glass to him across the tabletop.

Channing touched the glass. "Don't be concerned."

Leonardo made another garnish of olives, dipped it into his glass, put one into his mouth, and chewed. With acid rising in Channing's gut, he realized his grandfather had the same eyes as Channing—green, with dark eyelashes. The same eyes that Channing's rapist father had.

As though reading his mind, Leonardo said thoughtfully, "Moments like this, I miss my son. I used to discuss all business decisions with him."

Channing's jaw muscles worked. "Did you?"

"He died too young. Way too young. Never found out who killed him."

Suddenly, Leonardo wasn't an all-powerful Mafia boss anymore, but an old man stricken by grief. His shoulders rounded and slouched, and the wrinkles and lines on his face deepened, making Channing think of old leather. His fingers, touching the thin stem of the martini glass, shook. The man looked like a question mark.

Had Hakon grieved Channing like that also? A small needle of pain stabbed him in the heart.

He almost felt sorry for his biological grandfather.

Almost.

The irony was, Channing had been there, the day Hakon and Mia had killed Dan.

Channing's fingers tightened against the thin glass stem, and he was afraid he'd break it.

He remembered what had probably been the hardest day of his life in modern Boston. It was two years ago, in a Boston marina, where he'd watched Dan Esposito's yacht, knowing from his mother's stories that this would be the day she'd killed Dan...

Mom had been in the Viking Age for about a month, but then managed to return to the twenty-first century, determined to escape Daniel's network. But he had found her. And since he'd always wanted a son, he'd refused to let her go.

Hakon had negotiated with a Norn himself, who must have had a soft spot for Mia because she'd allowed Hakon to travel to the year 2019 to save her and beg her to come back with him because he loved her.

Channing had watched Hakon appear out of thin air. A Viking with an ax and a sword, he'd scared some people around him. Then he'd walked to Daniel's boat, where, Channing knew, Hakon and Mom would finally achieve what Channing had forbidden himself to do.

Finish Dan Esposito.

Leonardo met Channing's eyes. His gaze was watery from tears. "Something about you reminds me of him..." he said again. "So strange."

Channing's blood stilled. That reminder was all it took for a wave of revulsion to clear all empathy he had. Channing had been taught that honor was the most important value. An honorable man didn't rape or abuse women. An honorable man wasn't a criminal who made the lives of thousands of people worse through drugs and addiction. He wanted nothing to do with the Espositos.

Channing cleared his throat. "Again, you don't need to worry about a nuclear holocaust."

"Good to know." Leonardo raised his eyebrows and straightened his back, all vulnerability gone from him. He looked once more like an all-powerful businessman. "Well. In that case, I can make the reactor happen."

Leonardo raised his glass and cocked his head as an acknowledgment. He took a sip, set the glass down, and supported himself with his hands against the tabletop.

"But I do have a proposition. Your port. I want us to work together. There are certain shipments that my organization needs to come through customs undiscovered. I offer a percentage of the profits, of course. Five percent, just to keep your eyes closed and let certain containers come through without a check."

Not a chance in hell.

"I'm a man of means," Channing said. "Getting into the drug business has never been my ambition."

Leonardo took another sip of his martini. "You now have police on your tail, don't you?"

"So?"

"I have evidence suggesting that you may not be as oblivious about cocaine going through your port as you have led them to believe. Enough for them to arrest you."

He knew Esposito could manufacture whatever evidence he wanted. And the worst thing was, he had things to hide. If not for his time machine in the secret basement, he'd have said "Try" and walked away.

"And if I say no?"

"The evidence will find its way to the police. But that may be the least of your worries."

Channing threw back his third martini. Much to his Viking friends' annoyance growing up, alcohol had never affected him much. But Esposito didn't need to know that.

"So?" Leonardo said. "What do you say?"

Channing had only to stall him until he could make the time machine work. Then it wouldn't matter either way.

"Let me think about it," he said. "It's a lot to consider."

"Fair enough. You have two weeks."

"Right."

"But if you don't agree, or if you suddenly decide to work against me with the police, it will be *you* who's going to sit in prison. And in prison, there are always men who want to make a quick buck by shoving a sharpened spoon into another man's throat. The throat is a tender thing, Channing Hakonson. Norse descent or not."

SIX

Ella watched as a black SUV pulled up in front of the port gate, spit Channing out, and drove away.

If this wasn't shady, she didn't know what was. Channing had ditched their appointment today. His secretary couldn't reach him, which, she said, wasn't typical, and Ella had seen real worry behind the mask of professionalism.

Having finally given up on Hakonson ever appearing, Ella had left his office and been driving towards the gate. Now, she stopped the Taurus a ways back.

Distantly, she wondered if the secretary may be in love with him, although she didn't think they were having an affair. The thought of him being with the secretary or any other woman made her chest tense for some reason.

Channing staggered as though drunk, but stayed on his feet. He held his head and shook it. Was he hurt? She resisted the urge to open the car door and go to his aid. No. She'd better observe and see what would happen next.

Waving to the guard in the gatehouse, he staggered through a pedestrian walkway between the security booth and the red-and-white-striped boom gate. A tall gray fence surrounded the perimeter of the port, beyond which ran Summer Street, where a large parking lot and white office buildings were visible.

Channing was dressed in a jogging suit, and based on his disheveled man bun and rumpled look, she didn't think he'd showered today.

The guard left the booth and rushed to him. "Mr. Hakonson, are you all right, sir?"

Channing waved his hand once. "I'm fine. Can you please call me a cab?"

"Of course."

While the guard returned to his booth, Ella decided she'd never have a better chance to catch Hakonson off guard.

She opened the car door and walked over to him.

"Ah." He chuckled, his eyes shining. "Detective. Of course you're here. What time is it?"

"It's half past three," she said, and then, regretting it as the words were coming out of her mouth, "I can give you a ride. My car's right there."

His gaze followed her gesture. A lazy, satisfied smirk spread on his lips. "Right. Of course it is."

Against her better judgment, her heart beat faster. His barely noticeable Nordic accent added a melody to his sentences. She wondered briefly if that was how her mom's voice had sounded. She wished she could remember.

"I was on my way out," she said through gritted teeth.

"Your timing is impeccable," he said. He opened the door of the guard's booth. "No need for a cab."

The combination of his height, his muscular build, and the handsome roughness... He had a pantie-melting effect on women, didn't he?

Not on her.

Without waiting for her, he walked to the car and got into the passenger seat.

"So, where were you?" she said when she got behind the wheel and started the engine. The small space got even tighter, and she realized like never before how huge he truly was. His knees pressed against the glove compartment, and one shoulder rested against the passenger door. He had a distant look on his face, rubbing his stubbled chin. A whiff of his scent reached her —something earthy and musky, like a forest by the sea.

"Needed a day off."

The guard lifted the barrier, and she drove past it. "Why didn't you call your secretary? She couldn't reach you."

"Phone's dead."

"If you're as bad a smuggler as you're a liar, I don't need to worry."

He chuckled. "You have no idea, Detective."

"Where do you live, by the way?"

"Infinity Tower."

She scoffed. "Of course you do. Let me guess, the penthouse?"

He tsked. "Detective, Detective. Sounding judgmental is not going to make you many friends."

"I'm not here to make friends with you," she said. "Tell me you don't ask to borrow flour from your neighbor Scott Aler."

The richest player in the history of the Red Sox.

He chuckled, and she couldn't tell if he was joking or not. "I do. Aler is a good guy. Always has flour to borrow. So?"

"So? The richest people in the United States live high above the rest of us in skyscrapers and dealers are selling drugs to the most destitute right on the corner of your building. Isn't that perverse?"

His face darkened. "It is."

"What are you doing about it then?"

Glass and concrete buildings of the Seaport District flashed by as she drove.

The jaw muscles under his beard worked. The atmosphere in the car changed from playful to tense. "I'm not going to justify my choices to you. Or to anyone. You have no clue where I come from or why I work as hard as I do."

She hated men like him. Cocky, going around like the world belonged to them, like everyone would bend over backwards to run and do their bidding. Arrogant, self-righteous narcissist. Money was everything to him. She knew the type. *Massholes.* Boston elite, golden white boys coming from old money, with private islands and trust funds.

Except, he hadn't inherited anything, she reminded herself. He was a self-made man, had risen from nothing to everything.

Even worse. If he knew what it was like to be poor and have no help, shouldn't he want to help others?

She chose not to reply and tried to suppress her annoyance with him. They passed the bridge over Fort Point Channel, which had started to freeze on both sides. The Boston Tea Party Museum was brown against the gray sky to their right.

"I don't remember the channel ever freezing," she said. "Just look at that."

Channing glanced out his window. Frost had started to glaze the glass. His face darkened.

"Neither do I."

"Did you really spend summers in Iceland?" she asked.

Amusement lit up his eyes. "You remembered."

They'd just passed South Station and were driving into the Financial District now, the buildings growing taller, glassier, and whiter.

She chuckled. "Can you answer one direct question?"

He stared at the road in front of them like he wanted to burn it to ashes. "I don't like to talk about my past."

Hurt rang underneath the anger in his voice. His face was so tense, his high cheekbones looked sharp under his slightly bruised skin. Had the men in the SUV hurt him? Something softened within her.

"People who don't talk about their pasts usually have things to hide."

His glance at her was heavy and loaded with something she'd never expected from him.

Sadness.

Deep sadness, as if he were the only man left in the world.

Her heart lurched, sending an impulse through her arm to reach out and squeeze his hand.

But, of course, she didn't. She kept looking in front of her.

An odd movement caught her eye and she glanced to the right to three dogs standing between two buildings, panting, looking straight at her.

But something was odd about them. Gray and brown and wild looking, they didn't resemble any dog she'd ever seen before... "Are those coyotes?"

Channing followed her gaze as they passed. "Wolves."

"Are you sure? Saw a lot of wolves in Iceland?"

"Something like that."

"What's going on with the world?" she mumbled, looking at the start of another snowfall. A harsh wind threw tiny flakes onto the windshield. "Wolves in the middle of a city. Snow in October. Most of the trees are still green, for God's sake."

She should probably call the station about the wolves—they could be a danger, especially to the growing homeless population. But it would make her sound nuts, and she didn't need one more thing for Wilson to hold over her. She'd better choose her battles and concentrate on this case. But she could tell Ricardo. Maybe he would call it in or send someone to check it out. He was currently meeting with the FBI to see what information they could provide on the drugs and if they'd dug any details out of the captain of the container ship, who was still in custody.

Channing said nothing. The next traffic light turned red and Ella braked.

She should probably change tactics with Hakonson. Perhaps her full-on approach wasn't going to do her any favors.

"Two more blocks, then turn right," he said.

His tone was so icy, he probably spoke to Siri with more affection. The light changed to green, and she hit the gas, making the tires screech.

"Yes, sir," she muttered.

When she stopped in front of Infinity Tower, he sat for a few moments without moving.

"We have arrived," she said with a chuckle, and he smiled slightly. She tried not to notice his full lips. Thin lines wrinkled the small birthmark at the corner of his eye. A spot of darkness in the light, she wondered, or a spot of light in the darkness?

"Look," he said. "I'm going to be very, very busy over the next few weeks, so I'm not sure if I can be available anytime you have questions. I just need to change my clothes. So if you want to come up and wait, I can answer your questions afterwards. How does that sound?"

For a moment, she was speechless. There was nothing sexual about his tone, but the words sounded charged...like an invitation.

Like a man's excuse to get a woman into his apartment.

His eyes darkened and lowered to her lips.

She suddenly wanted to lick them—very, very much. But she couldn't. That would be an acknowledgment of something she knew was between them...this invisible pull to him.

He's a suspect!

But looking at his apartment might give her more insights and information.

She straightened her shoulders. "Sure."

He pointed at a gray metal garage door. "Parking's that way."

They parked in the underground lot and stood in front of the elevator. He was staring into space, and there was that sadness and that sense of loss she'd glimpsed when they were in the car. His hand, though far away, felt like it had a warm, golden electric field around it, and Ella crossed her arms over her chest to keep herself from reaching out to see if those strange golden threads might wrap around their clasped hands again. Surely that had been her overactive imagination.

He leaned against the wall with one shoulder. "How does one become a police detective?"

She arched an eyebrow. "Police academy."

The elevator doors slid open. The interior was sleek, modern with golden-gray geometric patterns covering the walls. He pressed on the button for the penthouse with a black electronic key, and the doors slid closed. The cabin smelled like sandalwood and jasmine, and although fifteen people could probably fit in here, it felt too small with Channing's big frame.

"I meant, you're way too gorgeous to be a police detective. Just curious if it helps you in your work or not."

The cabin stopped and the doors opened. He walked out into a dark lobby done in soft charcoal tones with abstract paintings illuminated by picture lights.

When she didn't move, he turned around. "Changed your mind?"

Although his compliment had left a warm and fuzzy feeling in the pit of her stomach, he wasn't the first man to hit on her. Her tactic had always been to let them know she wasn't interested. She wouldn't let a handsome man leave her flustered.

She straightened her back and followed him. "My looks shouldn't matter for the job that I do."

He walked down the hall towards a black door and opened it with a key. He held the door open for her and she entered.

She didn't know what she'd expected to see... Perhaps more of the same interior his office had: economic, contemporary design in masculine tones.

But the interior she saw was warm, and cozy, and inviting. The space was huge and completely silent, with a wall of two-story-high windows, beyond which, the snowstorm was now in full swing and had sunk the world outside into a sea of white, whirling waves. Hardwood floors reflected golden lights from geometrically arranged rows of industrial lamps suspended on black cables.

Between two L-shaped couches, one of which held a giant throw that looked like a brown bear hide, was a long, polished stone hearth with real fire.

A reclaimed wooden bar was on the one end, and a floor-to-ceiling bookcase filled with books on the other. The wall art and paintings looked Viking or perhaps Celtic—faces, animals, trees, and flowers woven into ornate patterns. Something about it reminded her of her mom's embroidery, Ella realized with a stab of pain as she proceeded into the room.

The space smelled distantly like fire, like leather, metal, and something woody and earthy. An odd combination for an apartment in a skyscraper.

It was so vastly different from her triple-decker with its tiny bedrooms, no closet space, and a cramped dining room. They lived on the first floor, and the hundred-year-old wooden house was alive with squeaking whenever one of the occupants of the upper two floors moved. They could always hear a TV murmuring, her aunt and uncle, or Rob's family talking. It smelled like old wood and food—someone was always cooking somewhere in the house.

Something was odd about this room, she thought, and then realized there was no TV. Who didn't have a TV in their living room?

Channing stopped in the middle of the room, and something about that picture felt complete. Like the core and the heart of the house was home.

Channing looked different here. Like a tired man who could finally take the worries of his day off and be himself. His shoulders relaxed.

"Mr. Hakonson," she said, "how does the security team decide which containers to scan? Is it at random or—"

"Drink?" he interrupted.

She almost said yes—it was so cozy and homey here, it felt like the day was over, and it was time for a nightcap.

"What? No. I'm still on duty. Can you tell me about the containers—"

He shrugged. "Suit yourself."

Without saying another word, he walked to a black metal staircase that ran along one wall and led to the second floor. Quiet stomping sounded as he climbed them.

"Mr. Hakonson?" she said.

Without looking back at her, he said, "We know that exotic fruit containers are prime targets of drug dealers, so they tend to get scanned first."

When he reached the second-floor landing, she realized he was probably in his private space. Upstairs, most likely, was his bedroom. And the thought of going up there, where he slept, took a shower...

Made love...

A sudden image of naked Channing came to her mind— bulging muscles, hard stomach, stiff cock.

Heat scorched her face. It was all in her head. The sooner she got some answers out of him, the sooner she could leave.

Angrily, she followed him up, her shoes clanking against the metal. "So why aren't more containers caught?"

"Expiration dates. Scanning takes time."

She kept following him, her shoes sinking into the soft carpet, and thought distantly that she should probably take them off because they must be leaving dirt. Transfixed, she kept staring at his broad back, his massive shoulders moving from side to side in a masculine swagger.

He took his hoodie off, under which was a simple white T-shirt. The backs of his arms bulged with muscle.

"What are you doing?" she said, slowing down.

"Taking a shower." He took the T-shirt off, revealing strong muscles playing under his skin on the triangle of his back. "Perhaps you'd like to help me?"

SEVEN

Speechless, Ella stared at Channing's ripped body. His hair was still gathered in a messy bun on top of his head, but more than a few strands had escaped. He turned to look at her with dark, hungry eyes, and her mouth went dry.

The hell she'd let him intimidate her with his muscles.

His gaze slowly traveled down to her chest, and a sly smile spread his lips. "Do you like my bedroom? Or do you like me?"

She crossed her arms over her chest and gave him a cold, hard stare. "Neither. Please stop sexually harassing an officer of the law. You're not doing yourself any favors."

With a chuckle, he proceeded farther into the room towards a glass door. Her ears burning, she scowled at him as he shoved his jogging pants down his muscular thighs and shook them off.

Ella's jaw dropped. She was staring at a perfectly round, gorgeous, white-as-snow, male ass.

He walked behind the glass shower door. "We take every precaution. Dogs, cameras..." He stepped out of sight. "I've even installed a finger-scan access system instead of a key card. Very expensive."

Now that he'd disappeared from her vision, she could admit to herself she'd never seen a man so beautiful in her life, except, perhaps in movies. Her ex-boyfriends were handsome, but...normal. Regular guys.

But this man... It was like he'd walked out of a magazine for Norse gods.

He turned on the water but said something at the same time.

"What?" she called.

He said something again, but she couldn't distinguish anything through the noise.

She walked through the bedroom to get closer, still regretting her shoes but knowing that if she took them off, it would further diminish the professional boundary that Channing was pushing against so hard.

She couldn't take anything off because he was already naked.

The bedroom was big and dark. Woody tones again here, with a giant, dark wooden bed by the wall. He had taken the Norse theme to another level here. Swords, axes, and round shields hung on the walls, shining in the dim lights. Another bearskin lay on the floor by the foot of the bed, and a white fur throw had been tossed over the bed.

What was it with him and the Viking stuff? Was it like a trick to get a certain type of woman into his bed? Or a fetish, like he imagined himself an overlord or something?

This was all so inappropriate. He was clearly trying to distract her, and she couldn't let him set the rules.

She was the cop. She had the power.

And she had too much on the line. The result of this investigation would determine her family's future, whether or not they would be all on the streets—and not just her immediate family, but the six other people who lived with them in the triple-decker.

She came to the door and pressed back against the wall so that she wasn't looking inside.

"Mr. Hakonson," she said loudly into the doorway. "Can you hear me?"

"Yes," he said through the noise of the water.

"This isn't working," she said. "You're being inappropriate, and I don't appreciate it."

Silence.

"I take all these distractions you're throwing at me as your insubordination during the investigation. When the police need your help to locate criminals, you find time to cooperate. End of discussion. Do you understand?"

Water splashing, then, "Yes."

"And if you don't cooperate, you're giving us reason to believe you have something to hide."

Water running. "I have nothing to hide."

"Right. Then I suggest that we meet tomorrow with no excuses, and you answer every single one of my questions."

"I will always find time for you, Detective."

"Good. Then I'll leave you to your shower—"

The water stopped. "There's a snowstorm outside, you can't go out in this weather."

Did his voice ring with concern?

"I can and I will. We'll meet tomorrow." She walked to the door. "I'm very close to finding a reason for a search warrant, Mr. Hakonson. So either cooperate, or we will leave no stone unturned until we get to the bottom of this."

And she had to.

Or she'd lose everything.

EIGHT

"Chica, what the hell were you doing in his apartment?" yelled Ricardo through the phone later that night.

Ella held it at a distance, wincing. She was studying a Google Maps satellite view of the port—more specifically, the building she thought was Mo5. There were several piles of dirt and two excavators next to the building. The date of the image was June 2014.

Seven years ago.

Seven years ago, Channing had become the CEO of the port. And where were they digging that dirt out of? There were no visible holes around the building.

"Calm down," she said. "I gave him a ride."

If there were no holes that meant they were digging a hole underneath the building.

"A ride? Why did he need a lift?"

Which meant, she needed to see what was in there. If they had fingerprint access to areas all around the port, it made key cards obsolete. Key cards were one of the most important methods that dealers used to smuggle drugs through ports. Often, they bribed port workers or stole the cards.

Often, they had a corrupt man or two on the inside.

"A very shady car dumped him in front of the port today. He was in his jogging gear. No phone. No car. Now if that doesn't scream criminals, then I don't know what does. He had to get a cab. So I gave him a lift."

She didn't mention that he had stripped naked in front of her in his apartment.

"I want a search warrant, Ricardo."

"Do we need one?"

"Even the port police don't know what's in building Mo5."

"Have you asked Hakonson to let you look in there?"

She sat back, frowning. "No."

"Might be worth a try. Then we don't need one."

"Hmm." She chuckled. "You're very wise at times, Ricardo."

He laughed. "At times?"

From beyond her bedroom door, something was banging and people were screaming.

"Ella!" her stepmother, Gloria, cried.

"Gotta go," she said and hung up.

She stood up from her tiny desk in her tiny bedroom, took three steps towards her door, and opened it.

The hallway of their apartment was full of people. There were so many voices talking and screaming at once, she could have been at a market. Her aunt and uncle from the apartment on the second floor and her cousin and his family from the third-floor apartment were here. Dad in his wheelchair and Gloria, too. Everyone shouted at one another.

Uncle Maurice and Aunt Cara waved their arms. Her cousin Robert, their son, made cutting gestures with the palm of his hand.

"...it's been six months!" cried Dad.

"...no work!" yelled Robert. "Where am I supposed to get the money? Pimp my wife out?"

Rob's wife, Stella, gasped and slapped him on the shoulder. "Language!" she yelled, bouncing their toddler, Pamela, on her hip.

"...when do we get a plumber?" yelled Aunt Cara.

"...do you really need to always wear heels..." boomed Dad.

"...garlic, like vampires threaten to move in!" came Gloria's voice.

"Ahhhhhhhh!" came a shrill scream behind Ella.

Silence hung in the hallway and everyone looked behind her. Ted, her twelve-year-old half brother, stood there, his hands pressed to his ears, his eyes shut tight, his mouth wide open as he screamed.

Ella rushed to him and hugged him, shielding him from everyone. She wrapped her arms around him firmly, but not too tight—something she'd read about how to deal with people with unstable nervous systems. The method was called Deep Pressure Stimulation, and it switched the body from running its sympathetic nervous system to parasympathetic, which helped to switch from "fight or flight" to "rest and digest" mode.

Ted opened his eyes, saw Ella, and stopped screaming, then removed his hands from his ears.

The silence felt almost as loud as the noise had been.

"It's okay," she said to Ted. "I'm here."

"Loud," Ted said.

"Yeah. They were loud."

"Sorry, bud," said Rob.

"La-la-la!" announced little Pamela.

"Why don't you all come in and I'll make coffee and tea?" said Gloria. "We can talk calmly, right?"

She threw a careful glance at Ted, and while the family

proceeded into the dining room and kitchen, she came to her son. Ella was still hugging him, watching the hallway sideways.

"What happened?" Ella said. "It's almost ten p.m. Why did they suddenly—"

"Ah!" Gloria waved her hand dismissively. "Your cousin Fiona couldn't shower because there was no hot water, so she flipped out. She has a rehearsal or something at school tomorrow. So Cara came to yell at your dad that he still didn't call a plumber or fix the plumbing because this has been happening twice a week now. Then Rob was on his way up and Dad yelled at him that if they all paid rent, the plumbing would have been fixed, and that the only ones working in this whole house are you, me, and Uncle Maurice. Then one thing led to another..."

Ted leaned away from Ella's hug. "Mom! Stop talking bad about Cousin Robert."

Gloria raised her hands in a peacemaking gesture. "You're right, you're right. You want me to tuck you in?"

"Yes."

Ella looked into his sweet face. "First give me good-night kiss?"

He beamed and pecked her on the cheek.

"Good night, Ted," she said. "I love you."

"Good night, Ella."

Gloria and Ted went in his bedroom, closing the door. Ella walked down the hall and went through the tidy living room, which was a sign Dad had strength to clean.

She entered the dining room where four adults and a toddler took up almost the whole table that stood in the middle of the room. The bay window gave a little more space, but it certainly felt like a cupboard compared to Channing's massive penthouse.

Snowflakes flashed in the darkness beyond the windows.

Though the storm had calmed since this afternoon, small snow-drifts lay on the ground. Ella would need to get up earlier tomorrow to clean snow from the car and scrape frost from the windows.

Dad was clanking with dishes and cups in the kitchen.

"Ella," said Rob as he saw her. "Do you guys have any jobs at the station? I'll do anything. Clean floors if I must."

Rob was a big man, fat and muscles combined. He looked like a boxer, although he'd been a mechanic for most of his life. The garage he'd worked at two blocks away had gone bankrupt last year. He had changed jobs several times since then. They couldn't afford day care, so with a toddler to care for and a baby on the way, Stella had to stay at home.

Ella's heart squeezed at the sight of dark-haired Pamela, who was playing peacefully with her mom's necklace.

"I'll ask, Rob," she said. "I hope they do. Keep searching—you're a good mechanic."

"Yeah." He rubbed his forehead, in the worried, desperate gesture of a sole provider for a big family. Soon, she may be looking for a job, too, if she didn't solve the case. "Thanks."

"Tea anyone?" she said. "Coffee?"

"Something stronger would be nice," said Uncle Maurice. Sturdy and with a big belly, he was always ready for something stronger. He was Dad's older brother, and even though he'd run an Irish pub for over ten years, he currently worked as a recycling collector. The pub had started losing money last year. Rent prices went up, food and liquor prices, too. Tourists couldn't afford to travel, and unemployed people didn't tend to splurge on dinner and drinks in a pub. There were more and more drunks on the streets nursing a bottle of home-brewed moonshine or a life-threatening cocktail of pure ethanol and water.

"Dad..." said Rob.

"What?" Maurice said, shrugging. "How am I supposed to sleep after this hubbub?"

"But you said you'd quit," Rob said.

"One won't hurt." Maurice waved his hand.

"You always say that," Aunt Cara said. "Ella, sweetheart, just water for your uncle, and I'll take chamomile tea if you have any."

"Sure thing."

How would she ever be able to look them in the eye if she was fired and tell them that they'd lost the house? Uncle Maurice fed his family and Rob's with his $27,000-a-year salary. None of them paid the rent, although their rent was so small it was laughable compared to the going rate in Boston. And Dad's mortgage, although twenty years old, had been arranged on a good cop's salary but set with such high interest rates that it was high even today.

Ella's income and the housekeeping money that Gloria brought in while Ted was at school covered it most months but left little to live on. Dad's disability check could barely cover the water bill.

And if she lost even that...

Her stomach twisted, worry burning in her gut. All three families would be homeless.

"You okay?" Ella asked Dad as she entered the kitchen. He was pouring water into the kettle.

"Yeah, honey," Dad said through a forced smile. "Why wouldn't I be?"

She took out the cups, sighing as she placed them on a metal tray. "That's what I thought."

He put the kettle on the burner. "How was your day? How was Wilson?"

With tension in her back, Ella opened a drawer and took out a box with a selection of tea bags. Then she took out an opened box of cookies and placed several on a saucer. How could she tell her dad that she could be fired in a couple of weeks? How could she say anything like that when there was nothing that he could do?

She knew he felt guilty for the years he'd been unable to work, even though it wasn't his fault he'd taken a bullet in the spine when a disturbance call in a bad neighborhood had gone south.

That had been ten years ago.

"Wilson's fine," she lied.

He turned his wheelchair. "I'm always here if you need any help."

"I know," she said as she hugged him around the shoulders. "Thanks, Dad."

The water in the kettle burbled and Dad switched the stove off.

"Let me help you with that." He nodded at the tray of mugs. "You get the kettle."

"Sure." Ella placed the tray on Dad's lap and took the kettle. Dad rolled his wheelchair into the dining room and was greeted by friendly "Ahs" and "Finally."

Ella placed the kettle on the table and helped Dad put the cups in front of their guests. The visitors picked their teas.

"A little bourbon would be nice," said Uncle Maurice.

"No bourbon for you," said Dad.

Their parents had been Irish immigrants, and although Dad and Maurice spoke Gaelic, or Irish as they called it, Ella and her cousins hadn't learned it, something Ella regretted. They still had distant family in Ireland, but had pretty much lost contact with them.

Uncle Maurice winked at Ella. "How's the job, Ella? Did you give anyone a good uppercut recently?" He made two fists, curled his shoulders into a boxing position, and hit an invisible target before him.

Ella beamed, pouring hot water into his cup. "Yeah, almost. You know I can protect myself, thanks to my uncle."

He'd taught her boxing from a young age. She remembered training with Uncle Maurice in the backyard. Unlike many girls her age who'd been bullied by boys who didn't know how else to get their attention, Ella had never been touched and was even feared by them. Everyone on the street knew she could break a boy's nose, because her boxer uncle taught her and her dad was a cop.

"You tell those bad boys Uncle Maurice is coming for them."

She laughed. "They all know."

"Yeah, and they're terrified, Dad," said Rob.

"You know," Maurice said, taking a large slurp of his tea, "folks are getting restless. What's all that about? Fights every night at O'Donnel's Pub. Demonstrations everywhere. Did you notice there are more druggies on the street than water in the sea? Christ on a bike!"

"And what about this climate change thing?" Aunt Cara said, chewing a cookie. "No wonder everyone's on edge."

Finally having poured tea for everyone, Ella sat down at the table as well. Pamela beamed and stretched her hands to her.

"Aw, come to your auntie," Ella said, delighted. She picked up the girl and placed her on her lap. Pamela tried to grab the hot cup of tea, and Ella pushed it farther away. Without anything interesting to explore, Pamela grabbed the button on Ella's blouse and pulled it into her mouth.

"Here's your bunny," Stella said as she gave her a toy she'd pulled out of her back pocket.

With the toddler busy, and her warm weight on her lap, Ella studied the soft hairs on her niece's head with a dull ache in her chest. She wondered if she'd ever have children of her own. She wondered if she was strong enough to hold on to the hardships of motherhood and not abandon her child like her own mother had. Was she even worthy of a man's love? Would someone stay with her through everything? Or was there something so fundamentally wrong with her that she didn't deserve that commitment?

Because even her own mother, the one person who was supposed to love her no matter what, couldn't.

Blinking a sudden onrush of tears away, Ella turned to Rob.

"Didn't you have a job after the port, Rob?"

"Nope. It's getting harder and harder to find something. I wish the job at the port had panned out. They paid well. I thought that would finally be the change in our lives we were waiting for."

Ella took a sip and put the cup on the table. "I remember the port fired you unfairly, but I don't know the details. What happened exactly?"

Rob waved his hand. "Started loading crates where I wasn't supposed to."

"Where?"

"A banana container—I started hooking up the container to be loaded onto the truck. It's midair, almost on the truck, then this manager runs to me, screaming. Apparently, I was supposed to be loading the crates into a minivan." He knocked on his forehead. "Sometimes I just don't think."

Ella frowned. "Was the minivan on the list?"

"No."

"Didn't it seem suspicious to you?"

He shrugged. "Don't know. I only worked there for two weeks."

"Did the banana container go through a scan in customs?"

"No idea."

"Were there more minivans lined up?"

He frowned. "Yeah. Come to think of it, there were."

"Do you remember anything remarkable about them?"

Stella chuckled nervously. "Ella, what's this about? Just some banana crates, he didn't do anything wrong."

"No, no, I know you didn't, Rob. I'm investigating drug smuggling through the port. Bananas and other exotic fruits are a typical target."

"Ah!" Rob said. "No. They were just white minivans."

"Do you remember the model?"

"Chevrolet Express, I think."

"And who was the manager that screamed at you?"

He shrugged. "Not sure. Never seen him before. I didn't know a lot of folks there yet, so that's not a surprise. But it was another guy who blamed me for losing the crates. You think they loaded drugs into the vans?"

She shrugged one shoulder. "Could be. Using someone new who doesn't know the proper procedures and then firing them—that's something smugglers might do to avoid detection."

Another indication that there was likely a man on the inside. She'd have a serious talk with Hakonson tomorrow.

And wouldn't get distracted this time.

NINE

Three days later...

DIRTY SNOW CRUNCHED under Channing's shoes as he walked farther down the dark and quiet alley behind Buzzed Rabbit bar. Despite the cold, a whiff of rotten food and something sour, like puke, reached his nostrils. Dumpsters lined the back wall of the bar. From the streets flanking the alley and the other side of the bar came distant drunk voices and the sound of traffic.

Condensation puffed out of his mouth as he breathed. Cold bit under his suit and shirt as he walked towards the dead end.

Earlier today, a message had come to his phone from an unknown number.

10 p.m. behind Buzzed Rabbit.

He was alone, a decision part of him regretted now. He could think of many places he'd rather be, like tangled in bed with the fierce little detective who seemed to be lodged in his mind and his fantasies.

Somewhere through the noise of the drunk pub goers, a rooster crowed. Once. Then again. Another rooster joined in.

Roosters? In the city? After midnight? Very odd. First wolves, now roosters. And this weather...

But before Channing could think more about how odd all this was, a shadow moved by the pool of light created by the bulb hanging above the back door of the pub. A man emerged, his shape a dark silhouette.

He was tall and slender, despite the puffy jacket. The man started producing a clicking sound—like the clip of a pen being hooked and released over and over. He had something round in his hand, and Channing stopped for a moment. Something was wrong. There was that chill at the back of his neck again, like someone breathed cold air on him.

"Hello," he said.

"Hi," said the man, and the clicking stopped.

The tone was rough and raspy, breaking like that of a boy whose voice had begun changing.

"Who are you?" Channing asked.

"Clicker." The clicking in his hand intensified. "You?"

"Channing Hakonson."

"Ah!" The clicking stopped again, and the man walked to Channing. His gait was wide, and he waved his arms like he was the king of the streets. "Hey, man."

He had a Southie accent and wore a Red Sox beanie. Deep-set eyes glittered under a wide, thick forehead. His wide mouth broadened in a toothy smile.

But Channing's attention never completely left the thing in the man's hand. In the gray darkness, he could see that the object was round, dark green, and had perfect square indents all around it.

Like a grenade.

Channing stayed completely still, a trickle of icy sweat snaking down his spine.

"What the fuck, man?" he said.

"What?" Clicker said innocently and dropped his gaze to his hand. "Ah, this little thing?" He held it up to Channing's face, and it took all the willpower he had not to jump back and run away. Clicker hooked his dirty thumb under a lever, pulled it up, and let go. It gave a click. He did it again. "Shitting your pants now?"

Channing swallowed. "A little bit."

Clicker chuckled. "Yeah. You all do. It's just a toy. Calms my nerves."

He held it out in an open palm in front of Channing.

"What do you need your nerves calmed for?" said Channing as he looked for any signs that the grenade might, indeed, be a toy and found none.

"Being a middleman for weapons, poisons, and radioactive materials isn't exactly the most chill job. My shrink says physical activity helps."

Channing sighed. This world. This godless world where moving a thumb was considered a physical activity... Try rowing a sixty-five-foot longship up the fjord for twelve hours straight.

"Anyway," said Clicker, looking him up and down. "You need a nuclear reactor."

Two roosters crowed in unison again, and both Channing and Clicker looked up and around.

Somewhere at the back of his mind, he remembered his father telling the story of Ragnarök.

Shaking off the strange feeling, Channing cleared his throat. "Nuclear reactor, yes."

"Hmm. Such a pretty boy. What do you need a nuclear reactor for?"

Ignoring him, Channing asked, "Can you get one or not?"

Clicker narrowed his eyes, then widened them as he looked Channing over. "Got any weapons?"

"No," lied Channing.

The clicking stopped, and the man patted against Channing's suit. His palm landed on the scramasax, and Channing cursed under his breath. Clicker went under Channing's suit jacket, and Channing grabbed the man's hand.

But Clicker's other hand flashed and something small and sharp pressed against Channing's throat.

"No weapons," Clicker said, breathing the scent of beer and hot dogs into Channing's face.

Helpless, Channing waited as the man removed the scramasax. Frowning, Clicker studied the blade, which shone in its unused perfection. Channing had had it custom-made by a blacksmith in Minnesota, a replica of the one his father had given to him as his first weapon. Norse runes were carved into the deer antler handle.

"What is this? Elfish? Like from *Lord of the Rings* or somethin'?"

"Viking."

The bare ridges where Clicker's eyebrows should have been rose towards the brim of his beanie.

"Viking?" He turned the blade in his hand. "Huh."

He put his own knife away. The grenade was probably already in his pocket. He stepped back, his eyes still on the scramasax. Helplessness weighed on Channing's arms. He hated being so vulnerable without his short sword.

Channing clenched and unclenched his fists. "So, can we talk about the delivery already and get on with our nights?"

"Sure, sure," Clicker said, then angled the blade so that it reflected the light, looking closely at it. "One week, it can be here."

Something released in Channing's chest, light and warm. In one week he could be out of here and back to his family. He'd be back with the Vikings. He'd hug his mother and shake his father's hand. He'd breathe the air of the North Sea, and finally, *finally* feel like he belonged again. Like he was among his people who knew him.

Like he was in his tribe.

"One week is great."

"It'll be delivered to your port. The ship has a strange name...*Naglfar* or something."

Clicker began running the tip of the scramasax under the dirty nail of his thumb. Hearing the name *Naglfar*, Channing felt his blood turn to ice.

He'd heard it many times in the Viking Age...in the story of the end of the world.

Ragnarök.

Naglfar was the name of the ship made entirely of dead men's fingernails. Led by the giant Hrym, its sailing would signify the start of Ragnarök.

His mind raced, and he remembered that even before *Naglfar* had sailed, the world had been plunged into the age of wolves. He remembered his father's voice, deep and solemn as he told the story by the central hearth of his mead hall: *The age of ax would come, the age of sword and wind and wolves...*

Channing had seen wolves—Ella, too.

...before the world dies.

Before Ragnarök.

Every Viking knew of Ragnarök like every Viking knew there were true gods and Norns and the world tree Yggdrasil.

The age of hunger. The long winter, Fimbulwinter. The world when brother killed brother.

All the civil unrest that was going on around the world fit the prophecy...

Three roosters would crow. First, the crimson rooster Fjalar in the forest Gálgviðr, then the golden rooster in Valhalla...

He'd heard two roosters crow just now.

And the third rooster as red as blood and as black as soot would crow in the underworld of Hel.

Could all those things be a coincidence?

He looked up into the sky. There was no moon, and he hadn't seen the sun after the snowstorm.

Clicker drew the tip of the scramasax under the nail of his index finger.

"And I'll need ten million dollars."

"Fuck."

"What?" He drew the tip under his third fingernail. "Too much? Sorry. That's what illegal radioactive substances cost you. Besides, that's a seventh-generation nuclear reactor. There are just three in the world, and this one was due to go to power up the Russian arctic station. But the project manager wants an estate in Florida more."

He looked up at Channing. "You have a week. Cash."

"Ten million is a bit too much. Six."

Clicker was on him before he could take another breath. His own scramasax was pressed against his heart, right between the ribs, in the place where with one good push, he'd be dead.

That was the moment he saw the true darkness, the true nothingness in Clicker's eyes.

"No negotiations, pretty boy. Ten million. You like Viking stuff, so you'll understand. You're bound to me now. We made a deal. Ten million or your life. Which is it?"

Channing gritted his teeth. This must be what Loki's eyes looked like. There was no negotiating with chaos. And Loki's children would kill the gods during Ragnarök.

As though to echo his thoughts, a wolf howled somewhere nearby. A chill ran over his skin, and not from the cold.

He had to get out of here. Money was no issue—he had it, and once he went back through time, who would care how much it had cost?

Channing nodded. "Ten million."

Clicker clapped him on the cheek. "Good boy. And this beautiful elfish weapon."

"No. The scramasax is mine."

"You have no power to negotiate, pretty boy. You've not only made a deal with Clicker, you're now in business with the Boston Mafia."

TEN

Sipping her coffee, Ella kept her eyes on Channing's car parked at the entrance to the back alley of the Buzzed Rabbit. This was definitely one of the dodgiest places she'd ever seen, and she'd seen her share of dodgy places, especially in the last year.

Ella had been doing surveillance on Channing all day.

It wasn't strictly authorized...well, it wasn't authorized at all. And she was afraid if she told Ricardo, he'd start lecturing her about breaking rules again.

But he wasn't the one in danger of being fired if the investigation failed.

Previous to this, nothing exciting had happened. Besides going to work at the port, Hakonson had gone to Boston University to give a guest lecture on Old Norse. He hadn't met anyone and hadn't gone to building M05 again.

But now he was meeting someone in a back alley. It was hard to see who that was. In the pool of light from the bulb hanging above the door, stood a tall, thin figure wearing a beanie. As they spoke, Channing looked back over his shoulder, his gaze gliding over Ella's car. She ducked. He scanned the street briefly but didn't seem to find anything suspicious.

Ella grabbed her camera and started taking photos. It was freezing outside, and Channing had no hat, no scarf, and his coat was open. Did he have an inhuman ability to stay warm?

The thin man made a fast movement, and something metallic glistened. Ella's hand shot to the gun on her waist, her heart slamming hard. It seemed the man had pressed the weapon against Channing's chest. How fast could she get to Channing if she had to protect him?

The two men spoke briefly, then the man in the beanie slapped Channing on the cheek, said something else, and stepped back. Channing turned around and walked to his car. There was that gait again—the dangerous predator on the lookout. The thin man stood, scowling at him, the long knife that looked like a short sword clenched in his hand. Channing started the car and drove away. Ella itched to do the same.

Should she follow Channing? Should she stay with the guy?

The guy, she decided. She knew who Hakonson was, where he lived, but she had no idea who this guy was.

The man walked towards the mouth of the alley. He stopped by a motorcycle that was parked next to the building and put the long knife in the back compartment.

As he replaced his beanie with a helmet, his bald head glistened briefly in the streetlight. He started his bike, the roar of the engine bursting through the empty street. Ella put the camera on the passenger seat and her hand on the keys.

But the man looked over his shoulder and straight at her. Slowly, he ran his index finger across his throat.

Goose bumps washed over Ella's skin as he turned back and his bike shot off down the street.

"Damn it!" she cursed as she started her own car and floored it.

She made a harsh U-turn and followed the roaring figure in front of her. Blocks and streetlights flashed by—the farther they moved towards downtown, the more cars there were on the streets, and she had to maneuver between them.

She first saw the rows of brownstones, the buildings growing taller and taller. And then, she knew something was wrong. The biker made a sudden turn into an alley on his right, and she didn't manage to turn in time. Before her, blocking the whole of Washington Street, was a wall of people. A crowd of protestors, shaking their fists and their signs.

She slammed on the brakes and her car stopped with a screech.

A loud bang followed from behind, and she lurched forward, her belt cutting into her breasts and stomach. She gasped, then twisted to look back, struggling to take in a lungful of air.

A blue car was plastered to the back of her Taurus. The mouth of the female driver was open so wide, Ella could clearly see a crooked tooth.

"Goddamn it."

Her first accident. She wished she were in one of her dreams, where she could rewind the events and relive them differently.

Spitting curses under her breath, she undid her belt and got out of the car. The air was loud with the protestors' rhythmic, angry chants. Wincing from the pain in her stomach and her right breast, she let out a long breath, condensation steaming up into the black air.

The vehicle that had driven into hers was an old Toyota, the front of which was now crumpled, as was the back of Ella's car. The Toyota's driver had gotten out as well, and stared at the damage with stunned incomprehension. Then she looked at Ella.

"But you were going so fast... How could you have just stopped?"

"Sorry, ma'am," Ella said. "I was—"

"But you were going so fast!" The woman's voice grew in volume, like a siren. Her eyes were wide, and her mouth curved down like a horseshoe. Ella saw the unmistakable signs of shock. "How could you have just stopped?"

The sounds of the protesting crowd were growing louder, also. It seemed the whole world was angry.

Ella wondered where the police were. Was no one supervising the protest?

An icy gust of wind threw harsh, prickly snow into her face and stole her breath. With it, she thought she heard the distant howl of a wolf.

The storm that descended as unexpectedly as an earthquake shut the woman up. A wall of snow attacked the city like an invading army. The wind was so strong, Ella had to hold on to her car or be knocked off her feet.

"Look, ma'am, I'm a cop," Ella yelled through the sudden wailing of the wind and the roar of the agitated crowd. "I'll take some pictures and write a report—"

"Fuck you!" yelled the woman bitterly. "You're a cop, huh?" she spat, wincing and blinking against the onslaught of the snow. "You just make everything worse. There's no justice in this world. Especially not from cops."

The woman got back into her car and tried to reverse, but by that time, more cars were blocking the lane, and the snowfall was so thick, it was hard to see anything.

"Ma'am, just get somewhere inside!" called Ella. "Here, there's a movie theater around the corner or the Paramount right here..."

The woman didn't move and began scowling at her from her seat.

Ella turned to the crowd. She bet it would be hard to keep protesting in this weather, not to mention unsafe. She huddled deeper into her coat and went to one of the protestors.

"Look, sir," she yelled into the ear of a young man. "The storm is coming. You should go home."

He glared at her with such hatred that she blinked. "Don't tell me what I should do! Someone has to stand up for what is right!" Just like Ella, he was blinking away the snow.

Ella sighed. She reached into the pocket of her jacket to call the station and ask if there were any officers on this, when there was a movement between the protestors, and the crowd spat someone out.

Someone tall, and tattooed, with a brown man bun and eyes like moss.

"Detective..." He squinted through the snow at her. "I thought it was you. Are you all right?"

She blinked. "What are you doing here?"

"I was just driving home when this crowd formed out of nowhere. They surrounded the car, and the cops are blocking the street to stop them from spreading. So I can't get home."

She looked over his thin suit. "How are you not freezing? It must be zero degrees."

"I'm usually in a car."

She sighed. "Okay. Come on. I can't let you freeze to death. My uncle's pub is nearby, and I know where the key is. It's been closed for a while now. We'll wait it out. And I can finally question you properly."

He nodded and she led the way through the growing blizzard. The idea of her and Channing, alone in the pub, started a warm and fizzy feeling in the pit of her stomach.

And suddenly she didn't want the blizzard to stop.

ELEVEN

Mo's was in a narrow alley behind the Paramount theater. In better days, it had been one of the unofficial cop pubs. It was secluded enough to be off the tourist track, yet close to Sudbury Street, where the police station was. But with the growing unrest in the city over the past year, the overworked officers no longer had the time or energy to grab a beer with friends after their shift. With a crushed spirit, Maurice had to close his beloved pub.

Ella retrieved the key hidden behind a loose brick near the entrance. As she unlocked the door and stepped inside, she shook her head and brushed snow off her coat. Channing stomped the snow and slush off his feet behind her.

The air was a little warmer here, still saturated with the scents of beer and bleach, though dust now tickled her nose, as well.

She went back into the utility room and turned on the lights and the heat. As she came back into the main room, pleasant yellow light filled the small space. There were six booths and a bar. The walls and furniture and even the bar itself were made of dark wood.

Sadness weighed on her. This pub—previously so lively, cozy, and popular—was a reminder of the struggle that her family and the whole world faced.

Determined to let some life in, she went behind the bar and muttered, "This is too quiet."

She found the remote control and pressed the on button. A Red Sox game with no sound came on the screen of the old TV hanging under the ceiling. Somewhere from loudspeakers, Disturbed played "The Sound of Silence," the rich voice of the singer crooning.

Very fitting for what felt like a small apocalypse outside.

Channing scanned the bar. "This place looks like it's been closed for a while."

Ella wet a clean cloth and wiped the dusty bar top. "Uncle Maurice's pub was never extremely profitable, but he enjoyed it and it did provide some income. But since last year, the bad economy ate up the whole profit. My uncle gave up the lease, but I suppose the owner never found a new renter. And it looks like they didn't know about the spare key, either."

Channing nodded. "Sorry to hear about your family's troubles."

"Yeah." She looked around the empty tables, the memories of her with Ricardo and other colleagues having a drink here, unwinding and laughing together, squeezed her chest. She shook her head. "What can I get you?"

He looked at the bottle shelf behind her. "There's nothing to drink."

She chuckled. "Uncle Maurice couldn't leave all the booze behind." She sank to her knees and opened the cabinets under the taps. "But it looks like there's a new Sam Adams keg he must have forgotten. How does a beer sound?"

"Good. Want any help?"

"Nope." She unscrewed the tubing from the old keg and put it into the new one. "I know how to run a bar. My cousin Rob and I helped my uncle sometimes."

She rose to her feet, washed two glasses, and filled them with beer. The scent of it tickled her nostrils, and as she walked towards a booth, the cool glasses in her hands, she realized the air was getting warmer.

She put the glasses down, then picked up the wet cloth and wiped the dust from the tabletop and the faux-leather seating that surrounded the U-shaped table.

As she took a seat, Channing joined her to her right and clinked his glass with hers. Drinking her beer, she watched him practically drain his glass, then set it back on the table. Something about seeing his big, strong hand with tattoos of Nordic runes on his wrist, the foam clinging to the very tips of his moustache, made her think he'd look more at home in some sort of warrior outfit, not in a tailor-made business suit.

Very sexy also.

She resisted the urge to jump up and get him a fresh pint. He could wait till she was ready—she wasn't going to cater to him like every other woman probably did.

This was a good opportunity to grill him. He wouldn't be able to avoid her questions here, not with a storm outside and nowhere else to go.

She narrowed her eyes at him.

"Right," she said, reaching into her purse and getting out her notepad and pen.

He frowned at it. "What are you doing?"

"What does it look like? I have some questions. And you have nowhere to go."

A lazy chuckle stretched one corner of his mouth under his

beard. He leaned back in the booth and looked at her from under his lashes.

"Neither do you. All right, Detective, shoot."

She cleared her throat, choosing to ignore his comment. He was good at creating distractions. She wouldn't let him.

"We've studied the container for forensic evidence and didn't discover any signs that this shipment was the work of a known criminal organization. The Boston Mafia specializes in heroin, not cocaine." Was she right or did a muscle twitch in his cheek? "The Mexican and Colombian cartels tend to smuggle cocaine through the US-Mexican border, so a container shipment through Boston isn't their signature. Though they may be trying something new. Still, this leads us to believe there might be a new criminal entity at play."

Or were existing drug runners trying to hide their identities by breaking their patterns? And then, there was the informant who'd told the FBI a powerful figure in the port was covering the smuggling.

Channing remained completely still and regarded her coolly.

She tapped on the notepad with her pen. "Do you have any reason to believe any staff at the port are involved with drug trafficking?"

"No. From day one, I made sure the security was strict as possible. I invest in training for my employees—they take container profiling courses, which allows them to identify the containers most likely to be used for smuggling. You talked to the chief of security, didn't you?"

"Ricardo did."

"Great. Then you know what measures we take and what is done to prevent this."

"We'd like access to the security footage."

"Absolutely. Anything you need."

"What about a list of all the trucks and vans that went into and left the port on August 23?"

"Sure. Why August 23?"

Of course Channing wouldn't know it was the day Rob got fired because of the shit show that was going on in the port. Either Channing was the reason for that, or he was above everyone and didn't bother himself with unjust layoffs.

Anger beginning to boil in the pit of her stomach, she laid her pen down and took another sip. She needed to be calm, so she did what she always did when she became emotional.

Stuck to the facts.

She leaned back in the booth. "Statistically, only two percent of all containers can be checked at customs. That's why seaports are popular among drug traffickers, because although some will be caught, most won't."

His eyes were narrow slits. His hands curled around the pint, shoulders bulged as he was leaning over the table, like a mountain casting a shadow. "Where are you going with this?"

She cocked her head, watching for a reaction of stress from him, some sort of a microexpression of distress. So far, there was none. "Once the containers make it through customs, the next step is the pickup. That's quite a bit more difficult. Port employees need to be bribed, blackmailed, or threatened. Lending a key card, forgetting it somewhere, picking up a duffel bag that's left somewhere in the port... The imagination runs wild and the sky's the limit."

His handsome face remained impassive, like a proud, Norse statue. "I might grow old while you're making your point, Detective."

She licked her lips, hiding a smile. He didn't know yet that she knew how Rob got fired. "And that's exactly where there's another crack in your facade. You had a temporary employee, someone who stayed for a couple of weeks only, who testified that he was instructed to load banana crates into unidentified vans instead of the truck that was on his list. Later, he was blamed by someone else for having lost the crates. He was fired the same day because of his 'mistake.'"

He gave a soft snort, picked up their empty glasses, slid across the bench, and stood up, half turned towards the bar. "But you don't know that there were drugs in those crates that your guy told you about?"

"Well, no, but—"

Walking towards the bar, he said, "So then there's no real evidence, is there?"

She opened her palms in a "How do you not understand this?" gesture. "There will be with security footage."

Standing behind the bar, Channing pulled the red Sam Adams tap handle. "Which you are free to have."

She gave out a laugh. "Right! Also from building M05? I saw you go in there, remember?"

His jaw ticked. He released the tap handle and set the glass down on the bar with more force than he should have. Beer spilled over the top and ran down the sides of the glass, and he sputtered something under his breath. "No." He picked up a clean cloth and wiped the glass. "You cannot have security footage from M05."

She scoffed. "You're digging your own grave, buddy. Do you even realize that?"

Complete silence was his answer as he took the second glass and pulled the tap handle without looking at her.

She turned to him with her torso and crossed one leg over the other. She was hot. Was the air becoming warmer or was it her anger at him? "Then I'd like to look inside."

He released the tap handle, picked up both glasses, and walked from behind the bar towards her. His heavy gaze landed on her, and something dropped in her stomach. "No."

She leaned against the table. "Do you not see how this seems suspicious?"

He put one glass before her and sat across from her. "I do not, Detective. There's nothing that concerns drug smuggling in that building, so it shouldn't be any of your business."

"Is that your official statement?"

"It is."

"What sort of renovations went on there in 2014?"

He drank a few gulps of beer, then licked his lips. "What?"

"Big, fat machines digging out tons of dirt. Construction vehicles. You'd just bought the port recently and then building Mo5 got a whole new...something. What was going on there?"

"Like you said. Renovations."

"Can I see any records of that? Renovation plans perhaps, orders, invoices?"

His murderous expression sent a chill through her. "This has nothing to do with drug smuggling."

"Then there shouldn't be any problem for you to show me the proof. Mr. Hakonson, if you refuse to allow me access to building Mo5, I will get a search warrant. And then whatever you're hiding there will be exposed. So I hope you have a good lawyer, because you may soon need one."

At her final words, he got to his feet and leaned closer to her, his eyes growing so dark they burned her like scalding water. The hair at the back of her neck rose.

TWELVE

"Is that a threat?" he asked. His voice was low and deceptively soft. Underneath it, there was a rolling thunder that made her core muscles squeeze.

Though if it was in anticipation, excitement, or intimidation, she couldn't tell.

Her heart was pounding like a fist. "A warning."

His gaze was boring into her. "I do not need warnings. And I do not tolerate threats."

Time stopped. At the thought that they were completely, irrevocably alone, the walls of the pub seemed to shift towards the center, ready to squeeze them both into an even smaller space. Air was sucked out of the room, and it was as though the lights dimmed. Somehow, Ella had the sense that nothing else existed outside of this moment.

A little shiver ran through her as he got out of the booth and walked towards her. Fire began roaring in her veins. His gaze held her captive, intense and dark and velvety. Good grief, what was she doing alone with him in the pub at night?

As if by magic, Saygrace started singing "You Don't Own Me," and Ella straightened her shoulders.

Because he didn't.

And why did she need a song to remind her of that?

The storm rattled the pub door, and the wind wailed in through the tiniest slits. It must be hell out there. Here, it was cozy and warm and...

"Well, fuck," he said, his voice crooning.

"What?"

"Where are you going to go with that weather outside?"

She raised her eyebrows. "Why would I go anywhere?"

Yes, he was sexy, and yes, she was clearly attracted to him, but it didn't mean she would act on it. Or let him seduce her.

He leaned over the booth on both his hands, towering over her. Ella met his eyes, and her breath caught.

He chuckled, his gaze slowly crawling down to her lips, then her chin, then her neck, then farther.

His voice dropped an octave. "Because I'm about to kiss you."

The hunger in his voice left her speechless. He leaned closer to her, and his scent reached her, making all her thoughts evaporate. Whatever he did or did not do in that port, whatever secrets he had, he was the most beautiful man she'd ever met.

His eyes settled on her mouth. "Tell me I'm not the only one feeling like my blood has turned into fire."

His words brought a vivid image she had had of him sprawled on his medieval bed, thrusting into her, owning her, like he'd come back from a bloody battle and she was his prize in a conquest.

Part of her knew this was bad. Part of her, the rational feminist and police detective, yelled at her to snap out of it and come back to her senses. Think of the consequences.

Play it cool.

"I don't know what you're talking about," she said, but even her voice betrayed her. It came out cracked and dry, and as she heard herself, even she could tell she was lying.

"Oh, yeah?" He reached out and tucked a lock of hair behind her ear.

As his finger brushed against her skin, a charge of sweet electricity went through her. "Liar."

She swallowed.

"This doesn't need to mean anything," he said. "No strings attached."

"I'm a cop. You're a suspect."

"No one will know."

Then his eyes became molten darkness. "I've never wanted a woman like I want you." He swallowed, his Adam's apple bobbing. "Ever."

And if Ella was honest with herself, she couldn't remember wanting a man like she wanted him.

As though reading her mind, Channing leaned down and kissed her.

His lips surprised her with their softness, their pressure light but sending a wave of tingles through her. Her mind blank, her lips parted, and his tongue dipped inside her mouth, caressing, gliding, licking hers. The kiss became demanding, and hot, and everything she'd wanted it to be. Soft, and giving, and hungry.

She was losing her mind.

No.

She pulled away. His eyes glowed with confusion in the semidarkness, as though the ground had shifted under his feet. But she had no strength to leave. When he kissed her again, turning her blood into hot lava, she couldn't stop.

Just one more time, one more kiss... But each brush of his

tongue made her knees wobble and her thighs clench tighter together.

Channing didn't seem to have the same reservations, his fingers digging into the back of her scalp, guiding her mouth where he wanted it. His touch full of sensual promise and electric demand.

It was like a dopamine hit. Her breasts were still pressed against him, her hands clenched tight around his thick biceps. Good grief, he was built like a Norse god and his body demanded worship.

The wind wailed, and the storm roared outside. Empty garbage containers rattled. Something knocked against the door, probably a box thrown by the blizzard. In the back of her mind, the part of her that needed this, *wanted* this, whispered to her to let go. To live in the moment for once in her life and stop questioning things when ridiculously hot, rich men started a violent drum beat under her skin.

He coaxed her lips apart with his tongue until he could plunder inside. He tasted like beer and something else she couldn't name and didn't even want to try. It was all him.

This time, he broke the kiss, but he didn't stop. Instead, he dragged his lips over her chin and down the long column of her neck. Each openmouthed nibble on her skin was accompanied by a husky whisper in a language she couldn't even recognize.

She let herself fall into it, the heady rush of his fingers on her skin, one hand still tangled at her nape, the other kneading her lower back as he tried to pull her into him tighter. She remembered how those muscles looked without the suit—at least from behind. The image took root in her mind, amping her arousal higher.

He stripped his jacket off, then made deliberate eye contact with her as he undid the cuffs of his shirt, loosened his tie, and stripped it all away.

Wow... She sucked in a breath and tracked the tattoos over his chest and arms. Some kind of primal pattern and so beautiful.

She traced the outline of a swirl on his upper pec.

"Your turn," he said. It was nothing less than a demand.

She didn't bother trying to deny him. She unhooked her belt first, the heavy weight of it, carrying her handcuffs, her badge, and her gun, and laid it on the scarred tabletop.

Did she trust him? Hell, with the size of his hands he could break her easily. And why did that flood her with a new level of hot awareness?

She stripped her long-sleeved shirt over her head to reveal the black sports bra underneath. For the barest second, she felt self-conscious about it. But when she met his eyes, they held nothing but heat as he traced the swell of her breasts straining the material.

"Off," he growled. "I want to look at you."

Knowing there was no way to remove a sports bra sexily, she tried for quickly and tossed the garment onto the growing pile.

He closed the short distance between them and took her mouth in a savage kiss. Nothing like the precise control he'd displayed earlier. It made her realize how much he'd been holding back.

But she didn't want him to. She threw her own need into the kiss, dragging her teeth over his lips, ravaging his mouth with her tongue as he tried to do the same to hers. There was no finesse, only sheer wanting.

She barely noticed when he lifted her off the floor. Nor did she think too hard when she wrapped her legs around his lean hips. Soft felt met her back a moment later, and it surprised her enough to release his mouth with one last bite.

He'd carried her across the pub to lay her on top of the pool table. Well, he was resourceful, she'd give him that much.

Once he'd deposited her fully onto the felt, he knelt between her thighs and stripped her suit pants down her legs. Then her panties followed. And suddenly, their entire situation became more real to her.

Except, he was no longer her suspect but a beautiful man intent on her every need. And she was no longer the cop investigating him but a woman who felt beautiful and powerful and wanted in a way she never had before.

And damn she wanted him badly in return. He dragged himself away from staring at her naked flesh and stripped way too fast for her taste. The end result was the same, though. All those beautiful otherworldly muscles on display. And that was how she thought of him right now, like her own personal Viking intent on claiming his prize.

With a gentle stroke, he started at her ankle. Trailing his roughened fingers up the backs of her calves, to the sensitive hollow of her knee, and still farther, until his hands met the curve of her ass against the table.

"No woman is more beautiful than you," he told her. No subterfuge, no guile, nothing but powerful honesty, and damn it, apparently godlike men calling her beautiful was her new kink.

She reached out, wrapped her fingers in his hair, and tugged him down to her mouth. The solid weight of his chest settled over her own, his hands skimming along her curves. One stopped at her breast, the other he used to brace some of his weight.

Gently, he rolled one of her nipples between his fingers, and she broke the kiss, dropping her head back on the table.

"Do you like that?" he asked. "Tell me."

Another demand. Another shot of liquid fire through her

veins. Anyone else and she might tell him to fuck off with all his domination, but with him, it felt right, and so good.

"More," she managed.

His lips turned up in a grin, and his fingers inched down her belly to where she needed him most. When his hand met her wet flesh, they both sucked in a breath. The hard press of his erection against her hip brought a new awareness to her.

He circled her clit with one finger but didn't seem content. Then he dragged two fingers down to her opening and gently prodded her entrance.

She clenched her eyes closed, her fingers digging into his forearm. "More, please."

"You want more?" His voice was husky with his own desire. "I'll give you more."

He fed his fingers into her body, then she felt him twist his wrist so he could press his thumb into her clit at the same time. She dug her nails into his skin, anything to keep her soul inside her body.

"I want you inside me now," she gritted out. "Please. Now."

She opened her eyes and his fire-filled gaze hit hers and he said the magic word: "Condom?"

She gestured towards the booth. "There's some in the back pocket of my duty belt."

He gave her a raised eyebrow but went to fetch one. When he returned, she shook her head, a laugh bubbling over. "I carry them to give to any working girls I find on the streets. To help keep them safe."

He ripped the condom open with his teeth, peeled the sheath from the plastic, and rolled it down his thick length. "Detective. How civic-minded."

Now, with him poised at her entrance, she didn't have second thoughts exactly, except for his size. She bit her lip as he braced himself on top of her again, this time the head of him nudging her opening and sliding inside so achingly slow.

Inch by inch, as if he had the patience of a saint, he pushed into her. All the while, she clung to him, her legs around his hips, her fingernails digging into his shoulders. Despite the stretch, she wanted more. Needed more.

Then, with a muttered foreign curse, he began to move. Slowly at first but then faster, until each of his exhales pounded heavily against her cheeks. She kept her eyes open, watching him, and he did the same to her until the pleasure washed over her, a tidal wave threatening to drag her under. Only then did she close her eyes and surrender. It was the moment he'd been waiting for.

He dragged his cock in and out of her faster and harder now, his thighs slapping against her own. The pool table underneath them groaned from the assault.

She held on to him, letting him take her harder, until finally, the friction over her clit set her on fire and the orgasm she'd been riding the edge of crashed over her. Wave after wave of sheer bliss sparked through her, only heightened by the heavy panting his breath made against her neck as he, too, reached his end.

His fingers were digging into her so hard she knew she'd have bruises, but she didn't care. Not with her Viking riding out the final pulses of his orgasm inside her. When he stopped moving, turning slightly onto his side to keep his weight off her, she studied him for any hint of regret.

In answer, he gave her a wide, disarming grin. "Had enough, sweetheart?"

The storm kept banging and thundering outside, like her heart, which had just given in to her darkest desire. Tomorrow reality could take hold. For right now, she wanted more. She grabbed him around the neck and dragged him back to her lips. "Who said we were done here?"

———

OUTSIDE, the snowstorm had been raging for quite a while. With the streets of Boston empty and still, it seemed as if snow had been the only living creature—attacking, intruding, smothering. It sang the songs of ice and loneliness, of life and death. It made white lace out of the city, which had been brown and gray and glass.

When the blizzard was sated and the wailing wind had begun to die down, three figures appeared outside Mo's pub, as though carried in on a snow gust.

The tall, broad-shouldered men stood in the middle of the alley, wearing long cloaks of fur. They looked around, blinking away the snow, round, Viking shields on their backs.

"What are those longhouses?" said one of them, pointing at the building flanking the narrow alley. "They are taller than mountains."

His long beard and braided blond hair caught the snow as he scowled at the other two. He pointed at the pub. "Do not get distracted. The Norn said he hides behind a red door under a three-leaf clover. That is where we go."

The wind died down, as though it had fulfilled its purpose in bringing the three Viking warriors. Despite the cold, bare muscular arms flashed under their long fur cloaks as they strode towards the door. Two axes and a sword glistened in the yellow streetlight as the warriors unsheathed their weapons.

THIRTEEN

Channing brought Ella to him. She was so sweet and soft and delicious now, all her thorns and hard edges smoothed after he'd fucked her twice. She smelled like that feminine, citrusy-sweet scent of hers, and now like him, and the Viking in him loved it.

He covered them both with her long coat as she lay on top of him, naked and warm.

Yeah. He'd told her this would be only once.

Trouble was, he didn't want it to end.

Now that he'd tasted her—knew how it felt to plunge into her hot tightness, how she tasted on his tongue, how she made him feel like he was about to enter Valhalla—he never wanted to stop.

Back at home, in the ninth century, if he'd met a woman like her, he wouldn't have hesitated. He'd have married her, offered her father anything he wanted, turned the world upside down for her.

A woman like her was gold. A goddess.

Treasure for a man.

But in this time, she was the opposition. She was hunting him, and she could uncover his secret at any time.

And he had to disappear from this world before she did.

The music had stopped a while ago, he realized. A cracking sound came from somewhere beyond the entrance door, and he raised his head to peer in that direction.

"Oh shit," said Ella, rising off his body, and leaving him cold. He swallowed as she stood before him, her beautiful breasts and narrow waist bringing hot blood to his groin again. "What's that?"

She picked up her bra and tugged it on. Unwillingly, Channing sat up and reached for his own clothes.

"This cannot happen again," she said as she buttoned her blouse.

He put on his boxer shorts, then the pants and started doing up his belt. He didn't want to hear that this couldn't happen again. "That's what we agreed on, isn't it?"

Someone banged at the door.

"Shit," Ella spat as she pulled up her pants.

Suddenly, all he wanted to do was lift her into his arms and carry her through the back door, make his way through the snowy streets to his apartment. Then he could lock them both up for at least a week and fuck her until they were both sore and as satisfied as cats after three bowls of milk.

He pulled on his own shirt, not taking his eyes off her face. The thoroughly fucked look suited her. The rosy cheeks, the puffy red lips, the eyes sparkling and glimmering, the utter relaxation he sensed in her despite the fact that someone was at the door.

"When was the last time you had sex?" he asked as he tucked his shirt into his pants. She gave him a puzzled look, and he chuckled. "Before tonight."

"Um..." Her face lit up crimson as she put on her blazer. "Was I that bad?"

He froze as he stuck one arm through the sleeve of his suit jacket. "You were phenomenal...absolutely perfect."

In fact, she fit him like a glove. No woman before had made him feel that. The pleasure, the heat, the incredible sensation of being alive.

Not in the ninth century, and not in the twenty-first.

Her fingers stilled on the buttons of her blazer, and their eyes locked. Heat ran between them, and they both wavered towards each other physically.

"It's just, I like seeing you so sated. So satisfied."

She bit her lip and bent down to pull on her shoes.

"Three years of drought will do that to a girl, I suppose," she mumbled.

Three years...

"It's been nine for me," he said.

She straightened so fast, her hair was in her eyes. "*Nine* years?"

He buttoned up his suit jacket. "Do you need to sound so shocked?"

She opened and closed her eyes looking him up and down. Then shrugged one shoulder. "You just don't seem like the type..."

"What type?"

"The loyal type."

Someone banged at the door again. "The loyal type?" He gasped. "You think I'm a cheater?"

He heard the hurt in his own voice and stepped back. He didn't mean to show her how much she'd actually hurt him. Him? Disloyal? He'd been raised by his father, Jarl Hakon, to be a man of honor, and by his mother, an abuse survivor, to respect women and their will, and to know it when he met a woman to hold on to.

She pulled her hair up into a ponytail. "I mean...no offense, but you kind of seem like the type that isn't interested in a relationship. Am I wrong?"

He clenched his jaw so tight, his teeth felt like they'd crack.

She was so wrong she had no idea.

What Ella didn't know was that he hadn't met anyone in fourteen years who made him feel like he belonged. Like he could be himself. He'd felt a glimmer of that with her.

For the first few years in this century, he could easily satisfy his hunger for women with one-night stands, but after some time, he wouldn't settle for meaningless sex just because he was horny.

He wanted more.

And he couldn't have more in this century because he'd find a way to go back sooner or later. If he fell in love, and worse started a family, he'd never be able to leave the woman he loved and his children behind.

"You're right," he said. "I am better off alone."

A fleeting look of something that resembled hurt crossed her face, but she hid it well. Channing wondered why she felt hurt if she was the one insisting this was just one time.

More banging came from the entrance door. Channing headed there, more to end the conversation than because he wanted to let anyone in.

He unlocked the door and opened it.

No one was there. Icy wind hit him in the face. The alley outside was white. Four inches of snow lay on the ground, on the fire escape stairs of the buildings, and on the windowsills. The snowfall stopped, and it was still and quiet.

So quiet, it didn't sound like Boston. It sounded like

another world. Like they were somewhere between realities, between present and past, between truth and dream.

The next second, Channing became very alert. He itched for his sword, which was in the trunk of his car. Someone had banged on the door earlier, but now all he could see were footprints in the snow. There were two or three sets leading to the pub door and then away into the darkness.

He cocked his head to the side without turning his eyes away from the street. "Stay where you are, Ella."

The snow was illuminated by the warm light of the streetlight. The windows of the buildings flanking either side of the alley were dark, as though no one lived in the apartments. Snow reflected white in the window glass. The air smelled crisp and fresh, like a new beginning.

Channing carefully stepped outside, snow crunching under his feet, the cold air biting through his suit and right into his bones. Step after step, he stalked into the street, careful and alert. But all he could hear was silence. The kind of silence that falls after a snowstorm, as though the world is asking, *What next?*

He had taken about ten steps when three figures strode out of the shadows and stopped in the middle of the street.

Their weapons glimmered under the streetlamps: the tall, blond man in the center and the man to his left had axes, and the third man had a sword, the blade a slash of silver against the white of snow.

As a crunch of snow told him Ella must have stepped into the street behind him, the three figures raised their weapons higher and stepped forward.

The light fell on their faces, and reality blurred around Channing. They were Vikings—from their clothes, to their somber, tattooed faces, to the unmistakable scent of animal fur, sea, and male sweat.

And they weren't just any Vikings. The face of the man in the center was familiar.

Eirik.

His old friend's left eye twitched as he studied Channing's face. Eirik looked much the same as when Channing had seen him last, only a year or two older. A few new scars marred his face, and there was more meat on his bones.

Shock washed over him, freezing his blood. Was he hallucinating? Without turning his head, he glanced sideways at the two other giant figures. He didn't recognize them. One of them had dark-blond, ear-length hair and was a giant—even bigger than Eirik. The other was dark-haired, the back and the sides of his head shaved in the manner of a Viking warrior.

That hairstyle was done so that the opponent wouldn't be able to grab the long hair and use it to take control of the warrior in battle.

"Odin's cock, you don't look like a Viking anymore," Eirik said in Old Norse.

The sound of the tongue he'd grown up speaking pierced Channing's chest like a spear.

Not Channing, he reminded himself. He wasn't Channing in Old Norse.

In Old Norse, he was Ulf.

"Stay still," he replied in Old Norse. "I need to make sure I'm not dreaming."

Eirik blinked. "Do it."

Channing took a few steps towards the Vikings and touched Eirik's cheekbone. Warm. Solid. A few facial hairs rough under his fingers.

They were really here. Three Vikings from his time.

He stepped back again, sensing danger. Channing realized he knew one of the other two men, Ragnar, although they'd never been especially friendly. The dark-haired man, he didn't know.

Channing shook his head. "How to Helheim did you travel through time?"

Eirik shrugged. "Norns. Spindles. You know Ragnar already, and this is Náli." He gestured at the warrior with the back of his head shaved.

Channing blinked, looking them over. Even though they looked real enough—and Eirik felt real enough—Channing still felt as if he were dreaming.

"What is going on, Channing?" Ella asked behind his back.

Fuck...

He looked back over his shoulder. She stood by the door to the bar, her hand on the gun in her holster, her face alert and alarmed.

"Ella, get back inside."

"No way." She took several steps closer. Her eyes skimmed over the Vikings and she raised her gun, pointing it at them. "Boston Police. Put your weapons down."

Eirik smirked. "A woman warrior. Fierce."

On impulse, Channing stepped between them and shielded Ella. "Ella, do not shoot."

"Who are these men?" she demanded.

"I know them, Ella," he said, then turned to Eirik. "Why are you here?"

Eirik looked him up and down with an amused half smile, and resumed speaking but now in English. "We came to stop a grave danger. A danger to the gods. A danger to the world."

Channing frowned. "What is it?"

"The danger, my old friend, is you."

FOURTEEN

Channing winced. "Me?"

Snow crunched behind him as Ella came to stand by his side.

"What *nonsense* is he talking about?" Alarm blared in her voice.

Eirik tossed his ax into the air and caught it to hold it in a better grip. The other two men took a step forward.

"See, Ulf," Eirik said. "I do not serve your father anymore. I serve King Harald. He worships the gods like a man should. Do you remember that day, when the völva came into the great hall of your father?"

Channing's pulse was pounding in his temples. His skin crawled, his blood chilling. He became acutely aware of how Ella went completely still. The rate at which steam was pumping out of her mouth slowed.

"The seeress told him of Ragnarök."

"Everyone knows of Ragnarök."

"Ragnarök?" whispered Ella.

Eirik slowly approached Channing, who began to back

away. "The völva told King Harald the Norns gave her a prophecy. She saw the end of the world. The end of the gods, just as predicted. Except, until then, even the Norns did not know who or what caused it. And now they do."

Adrenaline burned through Channing. His heart beat like a heavy drum. He couldn't feel his feet anymore, the cold numbing them.

"And?" said Channing.

"A man who tries to take destiny into his own hands and change the course of history. A machine that would allow him to travel through time at will. The man creating that machine will cause Ragnarök. As long as he lives, the world and the gods will die."

Channing's fists clenched so tightly, his short fingernails bit into his palms.

"You," said Eirik. "As long as you live, the world will die."

His mind raced. Yes, there were roosters crowing and wolves appearing right in the middle of a city. October in Boston had never been so cold—look at the snowstorm. The whole last year had been cooler than usual. And not just in Boston. The temperature was falling all over the world, an unexpected turn. The civil unrest could mean that part of the prophecy about brothers fighting brothers...

But it could also be explained by climate change and the toll that was taking on crops and other resources.

And yes, he was making a time machine, but he didn't intend to change anyone's destiny but his own.

"Okay, this is a fun story," said Ella, "but I need you to put your weapons down now."

Eirik's eyes flashed. With the speed of an attacking wolf, Eirik sprinted to her and knocked the gun out of her hand with the back of his ax. It flew somewhere to their right and landed in an open dumpster.

Channing met her furious, bright-blue eyes. "Run!"

The three Vikings launched at him without warning.

Channing ran towards the entrance into the alley. Ella ran in front of him, thank Odin. The dark, brick buildings flashed by on both sides.

But he was too slow. His damned elegant dress shoes slipped against the snow, making him lose his balance and stumble. His car—and the sword in his trunk—was about two blocks from here.

There was no time.

He wouldn't get far, not with this snow. He had to protect Ella. His only chance was to fight.

He made a sharp turn to his left, cutting off the three Vikings. They stopped, disoriented. He reached Náli from the side and shoved his fist into the man's face.

The punch was good, and Channing's hand hurt. He landed one more punch, making Náli's head wobble like a bobblehead doll's.

Náli's grip on his sword weakened, and Channing snatched it away from him.

Sword in his hand, he felt different now. The familiar but almost forgotten strength of a man holding a weapon surged through him. The feeling he'd had countless times on a battle-field, ready to protect his sword-brothers against the enemy.

Those were the times Eirik had stood by his side.

As though Eirik had the same thought, his blue eyes flashed before they darkened.

Channing remembered seeing this look on his face before. When battle fury took him over and he'd roar like he was ready to drink mead with Odin in Valhalla. To die the death of a hero. A death that would be remembered in legends.

Eirik was fighting for the world now. He fought Ragnarök itself. Perhaps, in his mind's eye he saw himself next to the gods, fighting Fenrir, the wolf who'd swallow the sun. Or the serpent Jörmungandr who'd kill Thor. Or Surtr, the giant who'd let the whole world burn.

Against the three, Channing wouldn't have a chance. He hadn't fought a real battle in fourteen years.

Eirik attacked, the snow crunching under his feet. He scythed the ax around in a large horizontal arc. Channing raised his sword, and the impact of the ax went into his bone marrow. Ragnar, who was in front of Channing, brought his ax up and over for a strike, and the blade caught the orange street-light and gave a fiery glare. Náli picked up two handfuls of fresh snow, rubbed it against his face, and retrieved an ax from behind his back.

"Leave him alone!" Ella screamed. Out of the corner of his eye, he saw her dive into the dumpster. "Where the hell is my gun?"

Channing deflected Ragnar's ax and ducked Náli's. But Eirik grabbed a black garbage bag that protruded from the snow and threw it at Channing. He hit the flying bag midair with his elbow, but Ragnar used the distraction and slashed across, the blade grazing Channing's shoulder.

His sword fell into the snow and he rushed to pick it up, but Ragnar kicked it away. The pain of battle burned him. Pain that he'd forgotten. Pain that used to be part of his life.

Joy spread through him. How sick was he that even this pain, the danger of being slain, of being killed made him happier than he'd ever been in the twenty-first century?

Ever?

He laughed, and the three men stopped midswing, glancing at one another quickly. His laughter ran across the silent city, the brick and concrete world. Among the walls as tall as mountains that suffocated him in the crispy winter whiteness, he felt more alive holding the sword than he had in fourteen years.

"You bastards," he said, beaming. "You think you came to kill me? You've reminded me once again of what I have lost."

He looked at Eirik.

"And you, sword-brother, who swore loyalty to my father... Look at you, traitor."

"I would betray your father before I betray the gods. So would King Harald."

Channing didn't care about King Harald. He was going back to the ninth century. He'd get the damned nuclear reactor. He'd divert the police. He'd do anything. This, here, was no life. Life was back in the Viking Age, no matter how many hardships faced him. It made every day more interesting than this safe, soft life.

Eirik raised his ax above his head. As the blade fell towards Channing, he stepped away and evaded it, then managed to go in from the side, grab Eirik's cloak, and throw him against the brick wall.

Náli attacked again, slashing the air before Channing with his ax. Channing jumped back, ducking each time the blade was right in front of his face. Catching a moment, he kicked Náli in the groin and ran past him. Ragnar was right there waiting for him with his ax at the ready. And this time, Channing wasn't as lucky. The ax landed on his shoulder, biting into the muscle with a blinding pain.

Channing groaned, momentarily confused. Ragnar attacked again, the blade of the ax flashing in the electric light. Channing stepped away but slipped because of his treacherous shoes...and fell.

"Channing!" he heard Ella's voice.

The quick crunch of footsteps in the snow sounded nearby, and before he could scramble to his feet, someone turned him over.

Eirik's face was above him now, eyes wild, brows together,

mouth in a furious snarl. It was the image of the perfect battle fury of a true Viking against the black sky. His arms with his ax raised high above his head about to land the blade and end Channing's life.

Time crawled. Pain receded. Even in the twenty-first century, Channing wondered if Odin was watching him. If this would count as death on a battlefield, a noble death from a blade. Not in a sick bed.

If Odin would allow the Valkyries to take his spirit and carry it to Valhalla, so that he, too, could ride with Odin for the fate of the world when Ragnarök would come.

The blade flashed down...

But it didn't reach him. Eirik froze suddenly and looked into the distance. He peered into the darkness, narrowing his gaze as though not believing his eyes.

The two other Vikings stood openmouthed.

Ragnar stepped back. Eirik and Náli backed away.

A howl came from nearby, and the whisper of snow under many legs...or paws.

Wolves?

Channing sat up, holding his aching shoulder. Warm blood flowed down his arm. The three men ran past an astonished Ella, turned the corner, and disappeared.

When Channing looked towards the entrance into the alley, he had an urge to stand up and run as far as he could. The strangeness of the vision was uncanny. In the glow of the streetlights, silver, gray, and brown wolves were running at him. Heads low, teeth bared, noses wrinkled, shoulders hollowed, as if on a hunt.

Channing pushed against the snow to stand up, but he was cold and light-headed and he slipped against the ice.

What to Helheim was this?

He raised his arm, ready for jaws to bite into his muscles, tear his throat apart.

But they didn't.

Fur brushed against his face, tails hitting him. Six wolves came to surround him. One of them started licking the wound on his shoulder, the others sat down on the snow and looked at something behind him. Channing blinked, wondering once again if he were dreaming.

"What the actual fuck is going on?" came Ella's voice.

He turned in the direction the wolves were looking. Ella was approaching, her gun pointed either at him or at the wolves. Maybe both.

FIFTEEN

Ella could smell rotting food on herself from the bath she'd taken in the dumpster, and that cut on her hand really needed some sort of disinfectant.

Strange things to think about when you held a gun on a pack of wolves that surrounded the man who, it seemed, was either the reason for a coming apocalypse, or just associated with complete lunatics. Lunatics who had spoken Old Norse, a language she had never learned and yet understood perfectly.

This man had made her come three times tonight. This man was a suspect in her investigation—and possibly a big drug trafficker, though deep down, she had a hard time believing that.

Did that sum up the situation?

No, not quite.

The wolves sat around him, panting like dogs, condensation pumping out of their mouths.

Channing looked around at the wolves. "Lower your gun."

She raised her gun higher. "You are surrounded by wild animals."

"The only one they seemed to be bothered by is you."

Was this true? It did seem they were very comfortable around Channing.

Slowly, with her hands shaking, she lowered her gun. One wolf whimpered, as though approving of this. Cautiously, Channing rose to his feet. As soon as he did, so did the wolves. They threw one last glance at Ella and then ran by her in a flash of gray and brown fur, and dissolved in the white mist of the city like melting snow.

Tucking her gun into her holster, she looked Channing over. "Was that your tame wolf emergency pack or something? Did you train them?"

That must be the reasonable explanation, she told herself, even though the image of her mother's embroidery and the wolves feasting on human flesh invaded her mind. It was impossible that the myth of Ragnarök would really come true, wasn't it?

As impossible as changing reality in her dreams...

She put her hand on his shoulder and turned him to get a better look at the wound. "This looks deep. Definitely needs stitching. Let's go to the ER."

His breath came out in clouds by the side of her face, caressing her. "I'm fine. Now that the storm is over, I can go home. It's only a fifteen-minute walk."

"Are you kidding? You can't walk anywhere in a suit in this weather!"

The sound of a revving engine made them look up. A yellow snowplow drove past the entrance of the alley, blinking lights bringing her as much joy as fireworks on the Fourth of July.

The signs of the civilized Boston she was used to seemed like they were from another world after the attack by three Vikings with axes and swords and a pack of wolves. Wild animals walking around Boston and protecting people seemed like something she'd read in a paranormal novel. Roosters crowing, winter hitting the whole globe harder than ever, people protesting and fighting one another, fighting authorities...

Her sleeping with a suspect...twice... What the hell was wrong with her? How could she have just given in to lust?

And how could she understand Old Norse? Had her mother taught her when she was too young to remember?

Channing shook his head. "Now that the roads are being cleaned, I can drive."

"Let me give you a lift," said Ella. "I'll just lock up..."

"Okay," Channing agreed.

Ella hurried into the pub, switched off the electricity and the heat, then locked it up and put the key back behind the loose brick.

Channing was already walking towards the entrance of the alley.

Ella hurried after him. "You're going to the emergency room, right?"

When she reached him, he said, "No."

"You're bleeding!"

"Then maybe you can stitch me up." He raised his eyebrows. "Can you?"

She blinked. Was he really asking her to suture him? Doctors treated wounds. "No."

"Then I'll do it myself."

She growled. "Why won't you go to the hospital?"

"Because look at the streets. In this storm, they'll have their hands full with people suffering hypothermia and frostbite... Besides, the protests usually leave people wounded and stabbed these days. I don't want to take the place of someone who needs it more."

She hated to admit it, but he made a crazy kind of sense. A reasonable, kind man. Could he really be a drug trafficker?

They walked out of the alley. Washington Street was empty, save the abandoned cars covered with snow—including hers. The snowplow had cleared the left lane, and she wondered if she could drive her Taurus out of the rut it now sat in.

Channing's SUV would probably have better luck getting out of the snow.

"So who were they?" she said as they walked down the street. "Those men?"

He glanced at her, his face tense. "Who do you think?"

She shrugged. "According to them, they came to kill you because some sort of a prophecy says you're the reason for Ragnarök."

He inhaled sharply, then exhaled a thick cloud of steam. "Yeah."

"What do you mean, *yeah*? You're not trying to say this was all true?"

They crossed a road. The engine of the snowplow revved somewhere ahead. The city, usually so loud and vibrant, was quiet and still. To her right, the cracked windows of the dark Starbucks blackened, reflecting a blinking streetlight. They passed by a bank with a boarded-up door and shop windows. Manic laughter came from somewhere above, probably through an open window, and the smell of marijuana reached her.

Great time for a joint.

Channing didn't turn to her. "What if it all was true?"

She grabbed him by the sleeve and turned him around to face her. His eyes were dark and wild, and he was still probably in shock—worse than she had realized.

"You cannot be serious," she said. "Are you saying you're also one of them—a time-traveling Viking or something?"

He stood completely still. So still she wondered if someone had pressed pause on time.

He turned away from her and resumed walking. "Let's just go. I'll tell you everything when we're home."

When *we're* home. Following him, she knew he didn't mean it like that, but a small part of her liked the sound of having a home with a man...with him.

They got into his car, and Channing maneuvered it into the cleared lane. As they drove through the snowed-in city, Ella saw that, slowly, it had started coming back to life. A man walked out of a building and got into a car, then followed the plowed lane. A couple appeared on the street, looking around as though trying to decide where to go.

Gathered around a fire in a large trash can, a group of people stood rubbing their hands and stomping from foot to foot. Others were visible, hiding in shelters made of plywood and scraps of metal. With a dark sadness, Ella wondered how many of them were still alive in the freezing night.

Channing was driving with a clear efficiency, not taking his eyes off the road ahead.

Somewhere, police and ambulance sirens sounded, and she knew Channing was right—emergency services would have their hands full like never before. They arrived in about five minutes and parked in the already familiar garage. When they walked into his penthouse, the warm air made her skin ache. She hadn't realized how cold she actually was.

How was Channing not hypothermic?

He walked into the kitchen and put on the kettle, which began its businesslike noise right away. "I'd offer you a drink, but alcohol is not a great idea if there's a danger of hypothermia."

When he laid the first aid kit in front of her on the couch, she swallowed.

He removed his jacket and started unbuttoning his shirt. "I can probably stitch it if you can't. But if you want to help, you could clean the cut first."

Pointedly looking away from his mountainous pecs, she walked to the kitchen sink. "Let me just wash my hands."

When her hands were clean, she returned to the couch and took the first aid kit.

Breaking open the pack of antiseptic wipes, she met his green eyes. "You could be a real Viking."

He chuckled, and she gently pushed him to turn his shoulder to her. As she wiped the blood from his wound, he didn't even wince.

She took out the surgical kit and unpacked the round suturing needle, threading it.

"Ready?" she asked.

She wasn't. Her hands were shaking, and she wished for a stiff drink. She'd never had to do anything like this. She was trained to give first aid, but stitching up a wound wasn't something she'd ever imagined doing.

He met her eyes. "Don't be afraid to hurt me, Ella." He smiled a soft, reassuring smile. "This is nothing. I've been through worse."

She blinked. "What have you been through?"

He inhaled. "Just begin. I'll tell you."

She cleared her throat, pinched the edges of his hot red wound together, and pierced them both with the needle. It took an unexpected amount of effort to get it through the skin. She felt him stiffen, and wondered how painful this must be.

"In Norse mythology," he said, his voice tight, "the three Norns are the beings that define the destinies of men and gods. One of those Norns sent my mother, who was pregnant with me, from the twenty-first century back to the ninth, to Norway. That's the Viking Age."

Ella stopped and stared at him to make sure he was actually serious. There was no sign of humor in his eyes. Maybe this was a metaphor or something to make some sort of a point. Shaking her head, she decided she'd wait to see where he was going with this and resumed stitching.

"My mother fell in love with a Viking. Hakon Ulfson. She decided to stay with him, and I was born there. Hakon is my father. Not by blood, perhaps, but by everything that matters."

Right. Great story... But despite her skepticism, the mere mention of Norway brought a tremor through her hands because it reminded her of her mom. Ella pulled the needle through her second suture. "No offense, but this sounds like fiction. Or a TV show."

Channing ignored her. "But my mother didn't think it was right that she had taken me with her—I was conceived in the twenty-first century, after all. So she made a deal with one of the Norns. Skuld is her name. It means, 'what shall be.' Or it can be interpreted as 'we reap what we sow.'"

She'd briefly read of Norns when she was researching Ragnarök, trying to understand why her mom was interested in that myth. Her pulse beat in the palms of her hands. Channing must really be in shock...

Ella shook her head and pierced him again; he jerked a little this time.

As she watched the black thread run through the hole, she thought this must be more and more painful for him. "Don't you have any painkillers?"

"Pain doesn't matter, Ella. Pain means I'm still alive."

Ella chuckled. "Sure, big strong man."

As she kept going, so did he. "My mother negotiated with the Norn that she'd allow me to choose by my eighteenth birthday if I wanted to stay in the ninth century forever or return to the twenty-first."

Ella pierced his flesh again. "So you're saying you were living in the ninth century among Vikings until you were eighteen?"

"Yes." His voice sounded like he had swallowed a toad. "But it wasn't my choice to travel to the twenty-first century. I had decided to stay in the ninth. My life was there."

Okay, she'd play along. "So...how did you end up here?"

"King Harald, as you heard, found out I was the reason for the Ragnarök. He ordered his warriors to kill me, and my family fought against them to protect me. The Norn appeared and said this was my last chance. That I should take it. And I did, to save my family."

That did fit his character.

Or maybe, just like her believing she was changing reality in her dreams, part of him believed he was born in the ninth century. Maybe he had dreamed it, too.

She looked into his eyes, and they connected. There were no walls. His eyes were open, and he didn't hold back. They had more in common than she'd realized.

There was part of her that did believe her dreams were real. And if they were real, could time travel be? Was he really a time traveler?

And was Ragnarök truly coming? Had her mother's embroidery been a warning?

No. The rational woman, the cop in her, knew the whole time travel idea was nonsense. Ella made another suture. "Right."

Silence hung heavy between them. "You don't believe me," he said. Not a question. A fact.

"No. I mean, it's a very creative story. But no. It doesn't even explain the wolves. Or how those guys got here, if they're from the ninth century."

"They said the Norns sent them here. And the wolves...

They are part of the story of Ragnarök. As to how they got to the city and why they were defending me—your guess is as good as mine."

She made a knot and cut the thread. "Done." Her work was rough and basic. His sutures looked like something from a horror movie.

"Thanks." He turned to her, so warm, and big, and so handsome. He could be a Viking warrior, she thought. He could be...

But he wasn't.

He cupped her face, his eyes locking on hers. "I know you don't believe me. But now you're the only person in the twenty-first century who knows the truth." His gaze was so soft, so tender, so...vulnerable. "I know you're investigating me, trying to learn if I'm a criminal. But know that now you hold the key to everything that I am. And with this information, you have the power to destroy me like no one else."

SIXTEEN

Three days had passed since the night of the storm, and Ella tried not to think about the fact that she'd slept with a suspect.

And that she wanted nothing more than to do it again. While she worked hard on digging through the evidence with Ricardo, she didn't see Channing. But every night, in her dreams, he came to her—all big and hard muscles and Viking tattoos—and for the lack of a better word, fucked her brains out.

As for the time travel thing... She had looked up the Norns on Google again and read about how the three sisters controlled destiny, but there was nothing in Norse mythology about time travel. However, she did find a Jarl Hakon, who'd had an unnamed wife. He also had a son who'd disappeared.

But that didn't prove anything. Channing might be trying to trick her or distract her from the investigation, or he might just have a rich imagination...like her. And all that Norse and Norwegian stuff kept reminding Ella of her mom, kept her wondering what had happened to her.

She didn't need this. She should forget about the time travel nonsense and concentrate on doing her job.

Trying to shake off the unwelcome thoughts, she unlocked the front door and walked in, stomping the snow from her shoes.

"—but this would cost a lot of money." Dad's voice boomed through the apartment from the kitchen as Ella opened the door.

Warm air full of the rich scent of cooked potatoes filled her nostrils.

"I don't care," came Gloria's shaking voice. "I don't care if I have to sell a kidney. You're not—"

A tremor of worry shook Ella. She released the door and it shut with a loud bang, making her jump a little.

"Quiet," Dad said, interrupting Gloria.

What happened now? She kicked her shoes off, and dirty slush still stubbornly clinging to them fell to the hardwood floor. Without taking her coat off, she hurried into the kitchen.

Brown grocery bags stood on every counter surface in the cramped space. The energy-saving bulb hanging low above the table in the center of the room didn't provide much light.

Gloria stood with her back to Ella, stumping a masher into cooked potatoes in a large pot. With her other hand, she wiped her eyes. In the darkened windows, Ella could see Gloria's reflection biting her lower lip, her eyebrows knit in a sad expression. Her slouched shoulders and the absence of an apron, which she never forgot, made a sour ball of worry form in Ella's stomach.

With a deep frown, Dad sliced onions on a cutting board set on the white-tiled tabletop. The lines around his mouth carved deep creases in the smoothly shaved skin—deeper than she'd ever seen before.

He looked up at Ella and pressed out a cheerful smile. "Hi, Ella. Shepherd's pie?"

"Okay, what's wrong?" she said, her feet filling with lead.

"Nothing." His voice jumped a little.

"Gloria?" Ella said.

Gloria didn't turn and kept mashing, using both hands now.

"Everything's fine, honey," she said in a nasal voice.

Ella undid her zipper and was pulling down her coat. "Is it Ted?"

Dad knocked the knife hard against the board, slicing through the onion. "Ted's fine."

Oh God.

"Is it you?" she said. "Something with your legs? Your spine?"

She hung her coat on the back of a chair.

"No." Dad kept cutting, the half rings of onion coming out uneven and messy.

Ella untangled her scarf from around her neck. "Gloria, you're crying, aren't you?"

"Don't be silly." Gloria managed a chuckle. "It's the damned onions, that's all."

Ella pressed her hands against her hips. They were not fooling her.

She grabbed a peeler, a cutting board, and the already washed carrots. She held the carrot at an angle against the board and pushed the peeler down. "You're both hiding something." Her hands shook, and the peeler slipped in the middle, the peel coming out thin and uneven. "I interrogate suspects for a living, remember? Even a child can see you guys are lying. Out with it."

Gloria threw the masher into the pot and covered her face with both her hands. She burst into sobs. Ella dropped the peeler and the carrot onto the board and rushed to her, hugging her shoulders.

"Gloria!" Dad thundered.

Gloria turned to Ella. "He has cancer," she said and pressed her forehead against Ella's shoulder.

"What?" Ella said, tears blurring her eyes.

Dad put the knife down, perfectly aligned against the side of the board, as always. "Gloria, we agreed."

He turned his wheelchair towards them. Gloria was shaking in Ella's arms.

"Cancer, Dad?" Ella said. Her chest hurt like a bomb had shredded it from inside.

Dad closed his eyes. "Yes."

"How bad?"

"It's bad." Gloria sobbed. "Really bad."

Ella wiped her eyes, fighting the waterworks. One crying person was enough. She had to get her act together and think positively.

She let out a long breath and asked as calmly as she could, "Where?"

Dad cleared his throat. "Colon."

"Stage?"

With a stony face, he turned back to the table and resumed cutting the onions. "Four."

Despite herself, Ella gaped. "Four?! That's— Isn't that terminal?"

Gloria sobbed loudly and shook, Ella pressed her arm tighter around Gloria's shoulders, fighting the painful convulsions that her stomach made, refusing to break out in sobs as well. Dad didn't say anything, his eyes pointedly on the task before him.

Gloria broke free from Ella, wiped her face with a kitchen towel, and gave out a loud snort, her eyes bloodshot.

"No point crying about it, is there? I've got dinner to cook."

Still sniffling, her hands shaking, she switched on the burner, set a large pan on top, and poured oil into it.

Ella swallowed the small, painful rock inside her throat. "So, what's the plan? Chemo? Radiation? What did the doctor say?"

Gloria stabbed the pack of ground meat and cut away the plastic wrapping.

"I don't think there's a point, honey," Dad said.

The floor shifted under Ella's feet. "What?"

Dad took the second half of the onion. "Will you pass Gloria the onion, please?"

He met her gaze. His steely gray eyes told her everything.

He'd made his decision. He wasn't going to fight. He wasn't going to be a bigger burden than he'd been ever since he lost his ability to walk.

Her arms cold and heavy, she took the board and passed it to Gloria. As she let the slices drop into the pan, the room filled with sizzling sounds. The scent of fried onion made Ella sick.

"Honey, will you chop the carrots, please?" Gloria said, her voice still thick with tears.

Carrots? They were talking about carrots when her whole world was falling apart? When she'd just gotten the news that her dad was dying?

But Gloria was right; in her usual kind, practical manner, she concentrated on the positive side of everything. Even ten years ago, when they had gotten the call that Dad was in the hospital, Gloria had cried a bit in the car on the way there, but didn't shed a tear when they arrived. With Ted, who'd been a toddler, cooing in the back seat and Ella, who'd just gotten into the police academy, Gloria'd become the strength of the family, a rock who'd told everyone they'd get through this no matter what and Dad would be fine—whatever that meant. The most important thing was that he'd made it through the surgery. That he'd live.

Ella should do the same. While her world was falling apart

yet again, they still had to eat, so the dinner still had to be made.

Ella sat in one of the kitchen chairs and picked up the peeler again. "Sure." She slid the blade along the carrot. Doing something useful was helping. At least she wasn't about to lose it. "You *are* getting treatment, Dad."

"There's no way we can afford it."

He was right, and he didn't even know how close she was to getting fired.

Ella peeled off another orange line of carrot skin. "I don't care."

Gloria stirred the onions with her spatula. "I'm with Ella on this. Money doesn't matter. We're talking about your *life*, Bryan."

His chopping gained speed. *Knock-knock-knock* went the knife against the wood. "It's too late for treatment, and I'm not leaving you with even more debt. It's bad enough Ella's carrying the mortgage and giving two more families a free place to live."

Ella attacked the next carrot with her peeler. "I want to talk to that doctor myself. Gloria, what exactly did he say? There must be some hope."

"There is always hope," Gloria said.

Dad slowed the speed of his knife. "There's no point of hope. He said the survival chances are minimal."

Ella looked up. "So there are survival chances?"

"Minimal." Dad laid the knife on the table and pushed the board across the surface towards Gloria.

She took the board and threw the rest of the onion into the pan. She handed him the board together with some unpeeled garlic cloves.

"I'll take minimal, Bryan," Gloria said. "I'll take anything. I'm not going to lose you."

*Not again...*hung the unspoken words in the kitchen.

As no one said a word, the sizzling of the onion and the rustle of garlic cloves being peeled pressed on Ella's ears.

Ella slid the peeler down the carrot. "Neither am I. You're getting treatment."

"No." Dad's voice rose.

Gloria propped her arm against her hip. "He did mention an experimental treatment."

"I'm not going to be experimented on." Dad put the clean garlic clove on the board and picked up another.

"Why not?" Ella said.

His lips pressed together in a straight line and he shook his head.

"Why not?" Ella repeated. She put the clean carrot aside and took another.

Dad suddenly looked up at her, his eyes the color of steel, raw pain thundering in them. "Because I'm not going to be a burden anymore. If this is the way out, then so be it."

The words hit her like a slap. She blinked, realization of what he was saying making her whole body limp. "Dad..."

"How do you think this makes me feel?" He pointed at his wheelchair. "I was a cop. I was a provider. I was a man. I took care of my family. Do you think I enjoy living like this?"

Every word hit Ella like a bullet. She opened and closed her mouth. Carrots, she reminded herself and, trying to stifle the shaking in her hands, resumed peeling.

"Stop this self-loathing," Gloria said. "None of us feel you're a burden."

He sighed and shook his head. "The point is, Gloria, I do not want the treatment. Not at this price. It's my life. And it's my death. And I will go as a man."

The carrot was clean now, and Ella felt like stabbing someone with it. Instead, she laid it across the board and began chopping. "There's no point arguing with him when he's like this," she said to Gloria.

How dare he give up? How dare he make this choice for the family? What about Ted? Doesn't he deserve to grow up with his father there for him?

"Exactly," said Dad as he started chopping the garlic cloves into tiny slices.

Gloria threw the ground meat into the pan, and the sizzling became low and intense.

Just like the anger within Ella. She finished with the carrots and passed the board to Gloria. As they exchanged a glance, Ella knew they were on the same side.

Good. Somehow, they'd get Dad to go for the experimental treatment.

They finished cooking the shepherd's pie in silence. Gloria always made double batches of everything because their relatives from upstairs would inevitably come to visit, if not that day, then the next, and they never said no to Gloria's cooking.

Gloria poured herself a small glass of whiskey.

"Can I have one?" said Dad.

"No. You need to be as healthy as possible. And I'll see about cutting meat from your diet."

"Meat?" Dad cried in horror.

Ella chuckled to herself. Cancer or not, some things never changed. While the two pans of shepherd's pie were cooking, Gloria started setting the table.

Ella stood up. "I'm going to see if Ted needs help with homework."

"Thanks, hon," said Gloria.

As Ella walked from the dining room into the hallway, the doorbell rang. She frowned, wondering if it was a late-night delivery.

She pressed the intercom button. "Hello?"

"Hello, Detective," said a far-too-familiar male voice through the static.

Her stomach clenched deliciously. The slight but unmistakable Nordic accent brought a heat wave that surged up her spine like a geyser.

She cleared her throat. "Channing?"

SEVENTEEN

"I like it when you say my name," Channing said, delight bursting through him at the astonishment in her voice.

"What are you doing here?" she asked through the intercom.

Wanting to see your face. Bury myself in you. Smell that scent of vanilla and citrus and something earthy and womanly. Spend one more minute in your company.

But it wasn't just that, he told himself. The delivery of the reactor had been confirmed; it would arrive in four days. Now that he had allowed her to access the security footage—of everything except for building M05—he was shooting himself in the foot by avoiding her. Because she knew about him being a time traveler, she had power over him, even if she didn't believe him.

He had considered telling her about the time machine, but he couldn't reveal the illegal nuclear reactor he was about to smuggle into the United States. Whether they'd slept together or not, surely a cop wouldn't let that slide.

And she was already suspicious enough. If she got a search warrant, they'd find his lab. They'd ask questions.

The reactor wasn't something he could easily hide. It would require careful preparation. It would require him to know when the cops would be in the port. And if he wanted to know that, his best course of action was to get close to her. He needed to divert the investigation. He needed to show her that there was nothing suspicious in building Mo5.

And if he had to spend more time with her, if he had to feel like he was breathing easier, like the very colors of the world around him had intensified, well, so be it.

He'd prepared building Mo5 for her visit, had hidden the key panel behind a fake shelf. He'd given Munchie and Georgina tomorrow off.

If he wanted to demonstrate Mo5 wasn't being used to smuggle drugs, the time was now.

"I need to talk to you," he said.

"How did you even find where I live?"

He had a pretty good computer guy. Pretty good meaning he could hack into the police system without raising suspicion.

"I have my ways," he said, looking up at the bright-orange triple-decker. The paint was old and chipped, but the dark-green window frames and ornamental trim made it look cheerful. The front windows on all three stories were lit, and the mouthwatering aroma of cooking dinner came from one of them. "Which I'd rather not disclose to a police detective."

She didn't say anything, and he stared at the white intercom, listening to the low static.

"Ella?" he said.

"Yes?"

"Can I come in?"

He was so curious how she lived. Was her home as warm and as orderly as he'd imagined it? According to her records, she lived with her father, her stepmother, and her half brother, who was twelve years old and had special needs. No husband or boyfriend.

At least not according to the official records.

The thought of her with anyone else lit his blood on fire.

"This is not a good time," she said.

"Can you come out then, please?" he said, brushing his hand through his hair. "This won't take long."

"Fine. But it better be important."

The intercom went silent. As he looked around the seemingly typical Dorchester street, he wondered if Ella had grown up here, running around the hilly street lined with white, beige, brown, and green triple-deckers hidden behind bushes and trees. Windows glowed in the darkness, orange and yellow streetlights illuminating porches and fences. The street had a sense of community about it, even though no one was outside. It was the sort of place where you knew your neighbor's business, and everybody knew yours. The sort of place where people got help if they needed it, gossiped, and borrowed sugar if they ran out.

The sort of community that was impossible in the penthouse of Infinity Tower.

The sort of community he'd grown up in in the ninth century.

Sadness stabbed his heart like a needle. With Eirik, Ragnar, and Náli, the past had reached out for him, only it hadn't brought the warmth of a hearth. It had brought curses and death.

Where were they now, the three Vikings? Were they surviving and blending in in this century? He remembered it had been hard for him, even though his mother had been preparing him for a while.

And why had they come now? Why not sooner?

From within the house, he heard a click and a thud and

light poured through the small stained glass window. Steps sounded from behind it. When the door opened, Ella stood in the pool of dim light.

She was still in her suit, her blond hair gathered back, exposing the natural beauty of her face. She smelled of citrus and her perfume, and of freshly made food, and his stomach clenched at the feel of home and comfort that she brought.

There was tension behind her mask of polite attention, and he wondered what it was about.

She arranged her face in a distant, official expression. "What is so urgent that you had to come to my private space?"

He chuckled, looking straight into her eyes. "There's no need to be so defensive. I've already been to your private space, don't you think?"

The blush the color of a bloody sunset that hit her cheeks was priceless.

She took one step towards him and held on to the doorframe. "I thought we agreed it never happened," she whispered angrily.

"Never happened?" He shook his head once. "I can never forget it did."

A flash of anger crossed her face, making her nostrils flare. "Channing—"

"I'm going to give you access to building M05 tomorrow. So I need you to clear your schedule."

She gasped. "You want me to just cancel everything and run to finally see what I've been asking about from day one?"

She was breathtaking in her anger. Blue eyes flashing and bright. He remembered her round pink mouth reddening as she called his name while he was buried deep inside her, bringing her to yet another orgasm.

His cock stirred again. He'd been blue-balled since the moment he met her. Yet another power she had over him.

Before he could answer, a door opened with a click behind her.

"Ella, dinner's ready," said a boyish voice.

"I'll be right there." She looked back and smiled warmly, the cheek facing him rounding so sweetly he wanted to bite it.

"Who are you talking to? Is it Nick?" The boy walked towards her.

Who the fuck was Nick? A boyfriend? The thought of her with anyone else made his fists clench and urged him to punch someone.

"It's not Nick," she said, and the sweet smile fell off her face and was replaced by a frown. The boy stood next to her and stared at Channing.

"Hello," the boy said.

He was dark-haired, unlike Ella. He was about twelve years old and had handsome brown eyes with the distinctive features of Down syndrome. Was he the brother Channing had read about in her file?

"Hello," Channing said. "What's your name?"

"Ted."

"Hi, Ted. I'm—"

"Leaving," said Ella firmly.

"Don't be rude, Ella," said Ted. "What were you saying?"

Something within Channing melted. Seeing Ted reminded him of his own younger brother, John, making his chest ache even more. "Channing. My name is Channing."

"Nice to meet you."

Channing felt his face spread into a grin. "You're very polite."

He sighed. "My mom."

Channing chuckled and looked at Ella. Her eyes shone with love as she gazed at Ted and rubbed his shoulder. The sight made something in Channing's chest contract.

"It's cold," said Ted, hugging his shoulders. "Do you want to come in? Dinner's ready. It's shepherd's pie."

Channing opened his mouth to say no, and he saw Ella open her mouth to say the same, protest written on her face.

But the scent of a homemade meal and the warm light from the window of the triple-decker made him think of the central hearth in his father's longhouse, where the family gathered to cook and eat and tell stories. The warmth of the open fire didn't compare to the love and acceptance of his family around him, joking and laughing and sharing stories.

He hadn't had a homemade meal for fourteen years. His housekeeper didn't count. It was her job to cook for him.

And imagining going back to his lonely apartment, as opposed to sitting at a table and eating with a family—even though it wasn't his family—made him open his mouth and say, "Yes."

EIGHTEEN

Inside the apartment, Ted removed his sailboat-patterned slippers. "You have to take your shoes off," he said.

Channing bent down and removed his shiny Italian shoes. "Sure," Channing said as cold seeped through his socks from the dark hardwood floor. The long hall was dim and crowded with a line of jackets and coats, a bookcase, and several sideboards where photos stood as well as an odd mixture of decorative items.

Ella came right behind him. "This is not okay," she muttered under her breath as she took off her own shoes.

Voices sounded from somewhere inside the house.

"I didn't want to be impolite," Channing said. "Your brother invited me."

She grunted. "Whatever."

Just then, Ted cruised through the arched entryway into the dining room, calling, "Come through, Channing."

Channing followed him through into a small, busy kitchen where a plump, brown-haired woman was setting a small kitchen table. A man in a wheelchair with dark-blond hair, blue eyes, and a straight jaw frowned at him.

The greenish-yellow kitchen cabinets were old, the brownish tiles on the walls chipped in places. Empty plastic packs had been separated from the small mountain of vegetable peels and from the paper wrappings. Even in these crazy times, this family was trying to recycle.

"Hello," the man said. "I didn't realize we had company."

The woman spun around and gasped. "Oh my word! Hello." She came to Channing, wiping her hands with a kitchen towel. She stretched her hand out and beamed a warm, welcoming smile. "I'm Gloria. Are you Ella's boyfriend?"

Behind him, Ella gasped. "He's not my boyfriend!"

The thought of being Ella's boyfriend heated up something within him and spread soft warmth in his chest. What was wrong with him? He never wanted to be anyone's anything. And based on how she insisted their one night never happened, neither did she—not with him. But if Gloria assumed he was a boyfriend, then Ella didn't have one. So who the hell was Nick?

"I'm her..."

Her one-night stand?

Her suspect?

Her nemesis?

"A friend," Channing said with a smile he couldn't contain, amused at her discomfort. "Channing Hakonson."

He was smiling more today than he had in the past fourteen years he'd spent in this century.

Ella's father stretched his hand out for a shake. "I'm Bryan O'Connor. Ella's dad."

Channing shook Bryan's hand. The handshake was firm and friendly, but Bryan was watching Channing with careful, estimating eyes. Ella had learned that expression from him, no doubt.

Ted's grin could illuminate the room. "I'm Ella's brother!" he cried. "I invited him," he announced to Gloria and Bryan.

Gloria ruffled Ted's hair. "Aren't you sweet, Teddy. Well, if it's us five for dinner, I think we should set up the dining room table."

Channing took half a step back. "I didn't mean to inconvenience you."

Gloria waved her hand. "Nonsense! We're the kind of a family that loves visitors."

Everyone helped to bring the dishes and silverware over to the dining room table, which was big enough for six people though there were at least eight chairs around it. The room was small and cramped with sideboards and cupboards along the walls, a couch with two chairs in another corner, and a TV hanging on the opposite wall. But it was clean and orderly and gave the impression that the family wasn't rich, but they took care of their things and saved them instead of throwing them away.

Ted went to the kitchen and switched on an old radio.

"...traffic jams in Portugal, Spain, and Italy because of snowstorms. Uncharacteristically cold temperatures were measured even in Morocco, Tunisia, and Egypt, countries completely unprepared for them..."

"Ted," Gloria said as she lifted a dish of shepherd's pie using oven mitts. "Switch it off. Channing doesn't want to hear that."

"Don't worry on my account," Channing said as he picked up several glasses and carried them to the dining table.

"...snow was seen in the Great Victoria Desert in Australia, where it has never been registered before. Hundreds of species are endangered as they're forced to deal with the weather. Scientists believe climate change has finally reached a magnitude—"

Ella went to the radio and switched it off. Ted gasped, his face showing astonished outrage.

Ella shook her head. "You shouldn't listen to things like that before going to bed," she said softly. "We've talked about it."

"Yes, but there's snow in a desert!" Ted said.

Fimbulwinter... The mighty winter that will last three years without a summer. The sun won't be able to warm the earth.

The age of wolves... The age of sword...

The three Vikings had announced Ragnarök was coming because of him. But even though they'd run away, he knew they wouldn't give up, and wolves wouldn't stop them next time. They'd be prepared for the wolves that kept showing up in the corners of the city and in the port, if the poor beasts even survived. Hungry people had started hunting the wild creatures.

There had been no more roosters, though according to the Ragnarök myth, they only crowed one time each, announcing the end of the world.

Ella came to Channing's side. "Are you okay? I can switch it on again if you're upset."

He shook his head and placed two glasses on the table. "I'm fine."

Gloria put a massive casserole dish full of shepherd's pie in the middle of the table. "It is terrible, isn't it?" she said. "Hard to believe there's snow in an Australian desert. I heard earlier today there were earthquakes in Hawaii, Iceland, and Russia."

She went back into the kitchen, leaving Ella to fill a plate with food.

"I'm not surprised humanity came to this," said Ella as she began cutting the pie with a wide spatula. "We knew for decades this was a possibility, although no one could predict how harsh and how fast it's all happening. And still we had to send more planes in the sky, and drill more oil, and drive bigger cars."

She handed the plate of steaming food to Channing, and he inhaled the most mouthwatering aroma. "Send more cargo ships that pollute the ocean?" he asked.

For three days, he'd been considering Eirik's words. Could the time machine really cause the end of the world? The nuclear reactor wasn't exactly the safest thing, either.

"That, too," Ella agreed without meeting his eyes, sliding a portion of shepherd's pie onto another plate.

Gloria came back and put a bowl of green salad next to Bryan's plate.

Bryan narrowed his eyes on him. "What do you do, Channing?"

"I'm the CEO of the Port of Boston," he said, meeting Bryan's stern gaze.

His face straightened. "Right. I thought your name sounded familiar." He rolled his chair towards the table and gestured to an empty chair. "Please."

"Thank you," Channing said, seating himself.

Ted sat by his side and lifted his fork. "Do you build ships?"

"No. I own the port where they deliver goods and can also get maintenance."

"Those big, big ships?" Ted asked, excited.

"Yeah," said Channing, unable to stop a grin.

"What's the biggest one you saw?" Ted said.

"There's one of the largest container ships in the world, *HMM Algeciras*. It can carry almost 24,000 containers."

Ted's eyes widened. "Twenty-four thousand?"

"Almost."

"I wish I could see that..." Ted said.

"Well, come over to the port and I'll show it to you personally. It's not at the port now, but there are other giant ships. Actually, why don't you come tomorrow with your sister?"

Channing met Ella's steely gaze. She finished serving and sat at her place next to him. Her thigh was so close under the cramped table, he felt his leg shift to hers like iron to a magnet. They touched, and a bolt of desire shot through him. Her eyes widened just a bit, and her pink lips rounded in a tiny, inaudible gasp. Channing swallowed as heat rushed to his groin. Odin's spear, he craved to take her into his arms, carry her out of here, and thrust into her and make her his.

Ted grinned. "Yeah! I have school, but can I come after?"

Ella shook her head, as if to free herself from a spell, and turned to her brother. "Hon, I can't tomorrow. I have to go to the port for work."

Channing hid a satisfied smile. So she would clear her schedule and come after all.

"I can come with you!"

Ella shook her head. "Sorry, Ted, it's work."

Channing said, "Any time is fine. Just let me know, okay?"

Gloria ruffled Ted's hair. "Isn't that sweet? Well, everyone, enjoy your meal."

She took her fork and scooped up some shepherd's pie. Channing took a bite as well, aware of Ella's and her dad's eyes boring into him.

But as soon as the food was on his tongue, he closed his eyes in bliss. It reminded him of the shepherd's pie his mother had made on special occasions. There was no oven in the ninth century, and everything was cooked on the open hearth or boiled in large cauldrons, but she made a version of it in a large frying pan with a heavy lid—ground meat with layers of peas and white carrots. And instead of mashed potatoes, she used mashed parsnips. Potatoes had only come to Europe after the discovery of America.

But this was better. This was a proper shepherd's pie that tasted of home, and love, and trust. That tasted like heaven.

Still chewing, Channing said, "This is good. You're a great cook, Gloria."

She blushed. "Not just me. Everyone helped."

Bryan scowled at the bowl of salad next to his already empty plate. "You know I hate greens," he said. "Get me more meat."

Gloria cut the soft shepherd's pie with a loud clank. "Well, you better get used to greens. If you refuse the doctor's treatment, you get mine."

The tension was as sudden as a draft from an open window. Smiles fell, hands holding forks froze.

Channing threw a careful glance around the table. Their faces were tense, worry suppressed under polite expressions.

Ted looked around the room. "Why does Dad need to eat greens, Mom?" he said through a mouthful.

Gloria forced out a smile, and tears welled in her eyes. "It's healthier, hon. Better for him. You should, too."

Tears? Was Bryan sick? She'd said something about refusing treatment... Why would he refuse treatment?

He glanced over at Bryan's square jaw, the stubborn, mournful set of his mouth with hard lines around it. Bryan breathed angrily, loudly. Channing knew plenty of strong, proud men, including his own father and himself, to realize Bryan couldn't be happy living in a wheelchair. Judging by the house and the furniture, the family wasn't well-off, so perhaps refusing treatment was about money.

Part of him craved to know what was wrong with Ella's father. He couldn't ask, obviously. But he had other means of finding out.

Ella was chewing her pie, her eyes bouncing between

Gloria and Bryan like two Ping-Pong balls. He could feel her worry, her fear, her pain. Pain and worry that he shared, too, being afraid to lose his loved ones. The helplessness of wanting to protect them from every harm and not being able to.

Only his loved ones were a thousand years in the past. Hers were right here at the table with her. So whatever had happened to Bryan, there was still hope to help him. And if it was a question of money, he had plenty of it.

The atmosphere at the table was charged and as thick as mud. Ted watched his father with a confused frown.

Ella put down her fork and leaned over to Ted. "Greens are healthier. I think we should all eat more salad. Not just Dad."

Channing chuckled. "Just don't overindulge in brussels sprouts."

Everyone stared at him, confused at first. Then Gloria burst out laughing, sprinkling Ted with tiny pieces of ground meat.

"Mom!" Ted protested.

"Sorry," managed Gloria.

Wiping his face with a napkin, she pressed a hand against her mouth and burst into loud, infectious laughter, tilting her head back. Bryan roared with laughter, and Ella giggled, glancing at him sideways and shaking her head.

Ted shrugged one shoulder. "What's wrong with brussels sprouts? I like them."

Gloria wiped her eyes. "I'll explain later, hon."

Ella leaned to him and whispered, "Fart jokes? Really?"

He chuckled, leaning towards her, as well. "I'm full of surprises."

Warmth spread through him as their eyes locked, hers sparkling with laughter. And for a moment, they weren't on opposite sides. She wasn't the cop who could uncover his secret lab, and he wasn't trying to pretend he was just a regular guy.

She was this beautiful woman with sparkling eyes and warmth enough to melt the ice around his heart, and he was just a man who got a glimpse of what it would be like if he could be himself, if he wasn't committing more crimes than she knew and bound to go back in time forever.

It would be this.

Joy. Acceptance. Laughter. Homemade food.

But it couldn't be. And him allowing himself to dream otherwise would only make the pain he'd inflict on her and himself worse.

He'd better remember himself and leave.

He broke the eye contact and returned to his food. From the corner of his eye, he saw Ella retreat and frown, staring at her plate. Regret stabbed him. But it was better this way.

The conversation returned to safer topics. The Red Sox. The Boston Celtics. Which teams the Port of Boston was sponsoring. Replying as quickly as he could without appearing unfriendly, he finished his plate, both dreading and longing for the moment he'd need to leave this house. If anything, he should be grateful, as it had reminded him of what he had lost in such vivid detail.

Channing stood up. "Gloria, I apologize, but I need to leave." He smiled at her warmly as she raised her eyebrows in surprise. "I don't remember the last time I ate such a delicious homemade meal."

Gloria returned his smile. "No girlfriend that cooks for you?"

Pointedly not meeting Ella's eyes, he said, "No."

He didn't want to continue this line of conversation and looked at Ted. "I mean it, Ted, just call any time you want to see a ship. If your mom and dad allow it, I'll be happy to do a personal tour for you. For all of you." He looked around the table. "Good evening."

He nodded and left the room under the distant "Byes." As he stopped by the apartment door to put on his shoes, Ella came to him.

"I'll see you off," she said and walked after him to the front door of the building.

He exited and stood on the porch. Huddling in her sweater, she half closed the door behind her. Crisp air was fresh against his face after the domestic warmth of the apartment. In the darkness surrounding them, with the silver light reflecting off the snow, she looked like an elf from legends, her eyes icy blue, her blond hair silvery. Her big eyes were on him, shiny and hesitant. He ached to reach out and brush his knuckles against her cheek. He ached to feel her soft skin under his.

"Thank you for being so kind to Ted, Channing."

Not Channing. My name is Ulf.

He wanted to hear his real name come out of her mouth. He wanted to confide in her, tell her everything. Today, something had changed between them. Today, he'd seen her family.

He wanted her to meet his family.

He swallowed what felt like a rock. "If I had a brother here, I'd take him to see the biggest ships in the world."

"Are you still insisting you're from the ninth century?" She winced.

Of course she didn't believe him. Maybe he should just let it go. Tell her this was all a joke.

He nodded with a chuckle. "Yeah. That night was crazy. Though I'm not sure which identity is better—a cocaine trafficker or a time traveler."

A small smile was born on her lips, and humor sparkled in her eyes. If he took one step closer and leaned over just a few inches, he'd find her lips. His body tensed, hot with longing. There she was, like a drug—one taste and it was impossible to quit.

All caution thrown like ballast from a speeding ship, he stepped to her, wrapped his arm around her waist, and kissed her.

Her lips were soft and pliable and so velvety, they could be flower petals. Her mouth was sweet, and delicious, and the moment he tasted her he knew she'd either be the end of him or be his salvation. With every stroke of his tongue against hers, he knew he'd never have enough of this. Desire like he'd never known before thundered through his blood, blinding him, deafening him, closing his nerves to all sensations but one.

Her strong, flexible body in his, the soft, warm mouth, the silky hair in his hand, the curve of her arched back. Through his suit, her soft breasts were pressing against him. Her scent was in his nostrils. She was grinding against him, her body in waves, and his cock stood at attention, and the more she slid against him, the hungrier he got.

There was just one thought in his head.

Mine.

This woman has to be mine.

To Helheim with it, with caution, with the law, with everything. She would be his, even for the few days they had left, because she belonged with him.

This, between them, was too good.

He withdrew, panting, staring at her, all pink-cheeked, her lips red and swollen from his kisses, her eyes so dark they were sapphires. Her gaze heavy on him, she touched her lips with her fingers, her eyelashes trembling.

"Three Loki's spawn," Channing muttered. "If you think this thing between us is over, you're delusional. It's only just starting, Ella."

He planted one final kiss on her lips, turned around, and walked to his car.

"I'll see you tomorrow," he threw over his shoulder.

She was watching him and hiding a small smile on her lips, and he felt a grin stretch his own mouth.

NINETEEN

As Ella grabbed the cool metal handle of the glass door to Channing's office and pushed, she knew she had dreamed this last night.

He was behind his desk, leaning over his laptop. All broad-shouldered, muscular, and tattooed, he looked up at her, and, unexpectedly, joy exploded like fireworks within her.

His eyes, pale green at first, gleamed with the same joy, then darkened when he quickly looked her over, head to toe.

He closed the lid of his laptop, and she had the immediate impression that she was his sole focus. "Hi." His low, velvety voice brushed against her.

Warmth surging through her, she closed the door behind herself. "Good morning."

Something was different.

Between their one-night stand, fighting crazed men dressed like Vikings, and him crashing her family dinner yesterday, he wasn't just a billionaire she had hated. Or just a suspect.

Or just a handsome man.

He was more. Though she was reluctant to admit it, he was so much more...

As he stood up and lazily walked towards her, the gaze he gave her was charged with heat and electricity, and...ache. The ache of longing and of unfulfilled dreams, and of something that could never be. Something that brought a shiver of recognition through her.

He leisurely sat against the edge of his desk and rolled up his sleeves, his forearms bulging, the hair on his skin light brown and golden. Damn. This was exactly how it had happened in her dream. "Are you being careful?" she asked.

"What do you mean?"

"Any sign of those three lunatics with swords and axes?"

"Oh." He cleared his throat. "I'm fine. I increased the security in my apartment. My sword is always in my car. I can protect myself. How's your dad?"

She frowned. "He's fine. Why?"

He stood so close, she could reach out and touch that heart-shaped birthmark on his temple. It was the color of dried red wine...dark and beautiful.

"I thought he was sick. It's fine if you don't want to talk about it. He's a proud man. You're a proud woman."

She was left speechless. It was like he was seeing right into her soul. Through her layers of defense, of protection against pain—the armor she'd built through the years. The strong police officer. The detective. The cop's daughter who learned self-defense before she learned how to drive.

A cop didn't get sick. His daughter didn't get seduced by a billionaire. What a cliché.

And yet, she was all that.

"He..." She swallowed. Channing had told her he was born in another century. She kept telling herself it was bullshit, but the part of her that believed her dreams were magical was curious and wanted to believe him.

You have the power to destroy me like no one else...

"He has cancer." The words were out before she could stop them. "It..." Tears welled up in her eyes, and before she could command her body to stop, a pained sob escaped. "It's terminal."

The wave of pain, of sorrow, of fear she had tried to suppress yesterday rolled over her. As another sob rocked her, strong arms like iron rods enveloped her waist, and she was pressed against a rock-hard chest.

He breathed into her neck. "Fuck."

She was a police officer. He was a suspect...

Warmth spilled through her body like whiskey. Instead of pushing him away, following the voice of reason, her stupid body took over. It already knew what it felt like to be in his arms. To be his. To be entangled around him like ivy.

And her body knew it was bliss.

She hugged him back, her arms wrapping around his hard neck as if she were drowning and he were a buoy. Her dad was dying. The whole fucking world was. She had to put Channing in prison, and yet she couldn't keep her hands or her thoughts off him...

How did any of that make sense?

"I'm so sorry," he whispered into her neck, his breath hot and wet. His scent—leather and the tang of iron, and that manly musk—wrapped around her like a protective shield. "I know what it's like to lose a father. To lose everyone you love." She went speechless for a moment. Was that an insane reference to him being a time traveler? His eyes warmed. "I wish I could take it away from you."

Something hot and wet rolled down her cheek from her left

eye. Great, now she was crying in his arms. "Don't be silly. You can't. No one can."

He cupped her face. His own eyes were watery. "I am trying to."

The place where he touched her burned and the muscles of her face went limp. "What?"

Without saying another word, he kissed her. The softness of his lips on hers brought on an immediate, urgent need that pulsed through her like the roar of a hungry predator.

As though he'd flicked a switch, her body took over. Maybe, if she hadn't been hit by the news that her dad was dying, and been such an emotional wreck, she would have stopped him. The rational cop within screamed at her: *What are you doing? Didn't you insist it would be only one time?*

But craving human closeness, the touch of a strong man, she wrapped her arms tighter around his neck and pressed herself to him. He locked her in the steely embrace of his arms and sealed out her fear and grief.

He pulled her to him like gravity. And who was she to defy it?

His lips brushed hers, and his tongue swirled around, sucking, owning, taking, as if he were dying and she was his last hope. Her mind went blank, and even the rational cop shut up. All she could hear was the pounding of her pulse and their combined heavy, ragged breaths.

Distantly, she noted a click of the lock and that the glass walls and the door turned milky. He must have some sort of button... His hands were all over her, tugging, grazing, caressing. Her breasts felt heavy and aching, and the only relief would be the glide of his naked skin against hers.

As though he heard her thoughts, he undid her blouse, lifted one breast from her bra and took it in his mouth. Wet heat surrounded her nipple, and as he swirled his tongue around her aching flesh, she threw her head back and arched into his embrace. A burning need spilled from the place where his lips melded with her flesh and shot straight to her core.

Her panties were drenched right away, and as he took her second breast from her bra with his other hand and began circling her nipple with his thumb, she felt her deep inner muscles clench deliciously.

"Channing..." she whispered.

"Shhh, *elskan min*," he murmured against her skin, sending a vibration through her. "I couldn't stop thinking of you for a moment..."

He couldn't stop thinking about her? *Elskan min.* He was calling her his darling, she realized. How...?

All thoughts fled as he left her breasts and began making his way down her naked stomach. Then he undid her suit pants, scalding the skin of her pelvis with his hot breath. Her legs went weak and boneless, and she had to hold on to his shoulders.

He pulled her panties down her legs, leaving a wet trace along her inner thigh. "Thinking of you every fucking minute."

She shivered, unsure if she should be embarrassed, but he growled like a wolf, setting fire to all her inhibitions.

"Fucking you," he said and stood up, lifting her by her ass and setting her on the desk. "Eating you." His eyes were almost black as he met her gaze, wild with desire. "Making you come. Over and over and over again."

She gasped as he fell to his knees in front of her and spread her legs before his face. Wow, this was...*hot.* They were in blinding, broad daylight. He could see all of her—the unshaved, unwaxed her, because it had been so long since she'd had a boyfriend.

"Fuck..." he growled as his intense eyes took in her folds. "You're so ready for me."

Before she could reply, his mouth was on her, and she gasped out a cry as pleasure shot through her in all directions. He swirled his tongue gently around and around and around the perimeter, spilling liquid fire through her veins, teasing her. Then he found the center of her pleasure, that needy, throbbing bud, and flicked it with his tongue, softly—once...twice...

The wave of pleasure started building within her, and she clenched her inner muscles. How could he know that this teasing was just what she needed?

But he withdrew, and she opened her eyes, panting, watching him watching her.

He growled again. "You'll be the death of me, Ella..." he said, looking her over. "If we lived in a different time... If we weren't on opposite sides of this investigation... I'd have married you by now."

Married her? The daze of her arousal was cushioning her from the full impact of his words and what they meant. While he was unzipping his pants, her mind raced. What modern man talked like that?

But all questions were kicked out of her head by the jutting erection that sprang from his boxer briefs, thick and hard and so big she lost her breath.

She wanted it inside her. As he broke the wrapping of a condom and rolled it on, all she could think about was how she wanted him to stretch her, and fill her, and make her explode and contract and...

He positioned himself against her, nudging against her entrance, his thick erection sliding against her oversensitive flesh, taking her swelling and sweet throbbing to the next level. He kissed her again, his tongue dancing around hers in a worshipping but possessive way, causing another wave of wetness to spill from her entrance. She groaned, impatient now, and wrapped her legs around his hips, urging him to enter her.

Slowly, slowly, he eased himself inside of her...the bastard! He was bringing her so much more pleasure—teasing her, giving her a galaxy of sensations, and yet not enough to bring her the release that was so close.

When he was so deep inside her that he was stretching her to the limit, he groaned.

"Fuck, you feel so good," he growled into her ear. Then he looked into her eyes, and for the first time ever, she saw no shields of protection. No armor. No lies. "If I had to cross centuries to find you, it was all worth it. You're a dream, Ella."

Tears welled in her eyes, because for just a moment she believed him. She heard him saying how it all was. He had crossed centuries. And he did love her. Love? He hadn't even said the word. Where had that come from?

But he started moving within her, and all thoughts evaporated as the delicious friction of his cock conquered her whole. He pounded in and out of her faster and faster, and something clunked and spilled on his desk. Stuff fell on the floor, hitting, breaking, but all she could hear were her moans and his growls.

Closer and closer he was bringing her towards the edge, and as a blinding, hot pleasure rushed through her like a volcanic eruption, and sweet contractions took over her world, he stiffened against her, giving a tortured groan. As she was shaking in his arms in the aftershocks, he buried his face in her hair. They breathed in one rhythm, their hearts beating in unison.

Then cold reality started to seep in.

Yet again, she had broken the ethics of a police detective. She went completely still under his gaze.

"What?" he said.

She shook her head, not looking at him, and tried to free herself, but he held her in his arms. "What is it, Ella?"

She sighed. "I'm an idiot, that's what."

He hooked his finger under her chin and gently raised her face, making her look at him. When she met his green eyes, there was nothing but light in his gaze. "Is it about the investigation?"

"Of course it's about the investigation. Nothing has changed. I'm still a cop and you're still a suspect. I can't sleep with you. I can't have any sort of relationship with you. Or I'll be in deep trouble. You have no idea."

He let out a long breath and his eyes grew solemn and resolute. "You don't have to worry, Ella. I promise you. Whatever happens, I swear to you on everything that's dear to me, I'd rather die than say a word about us."

He was so serious, so solemn, as though he were taking a blood oath in front of a king. Warmth spread through her heart. Could she really trust him?

"Even if you're under oath in a courtroom?" she asked.

"I am under oath. Under oath to you. Anything else doesn't matter. A courtroom means nothing to me. You mean everything."

Her mouth went dry, and her throat scratched. No one had ever said anything remotely like that to her. No man had ever cared about her like he did. But she knew what it was like to be abandoned. And she couldn't trust him completely...could she?

And as she slid from his embrace, and searched for her panties on the floor, she suddenly stood completely still as reality blurred and slowed.

She had dreamed about *exactly* this last night. The wild, animalistic sex in his office. He'd said the exact same words and done the exact same things.

Only, at the end of her dream, she'd told him that she didn't believe him and that this really would never happen again.

And now, she just couldn't bring herself to say that.

Like an addict who knew she was making a bad choice, she still wanted more.

As she was pulling her pants up, her phone rang. "Hello?" she said without looking, glad for a distraction.

"Ella!" It was Gloria, her voice agitated. "Are you at the port already?"

"Yes. Why?"

"Ted's therapist is sick and they have no substitute, so I'm bringing him to you."

"What? Why? I'm about to look at a possible crime scene, to search for evidence. He can't come with—"

"Make it happen, hon. I just got a call from the hospital. Your father has been accepted to the experimental treatment program."

The floor shifted under Ella's feet.

"What? How?"

"An anonymous donor sponsored him. Donated half a million dollars."

Confused, refusing to allow hope to take her over, Ella locked her eyes with Channing, who was buttoning up his pants, dark eyes observing her from under his lashes.

"But..." Ella said. "This must be some mistake?"

"I know. Hard to believe..."

"If something sounds too good to be true, it is!" growled Ella's dad in the background.

"Okay," Ella said, her heart pounding. "When will you be here?"

"Half an hour, I think. We're all in the car already and on our way. Your dad and I need to go to Mass Gen right away."

Half an hour would give Ella the chance to look around building Mo5 before Ted got there.

"I'll pick him up at the gates."

As she hung up the phone, she wondered if the anonymous

donor was Channing. Who else had known her dad was sick and had enough money to donate half a million?

If her suspect had anything to do with this, it could be considered a bribe.

She was further entangling herself with this man. This kind, Viking sex god with a heart of gold and arms of a warrior.

Did she care that every day she was digging a grave for her career?

Or was she ready to do anything as long as her dad had a chance to live?

TWENTY

The door to building M05 opened with a gnash, and Ella's heart jumped a little. What was she expecting? A freaking monster to jump on her?

Cold seeped over her from the darkness beyond the door. Channing was holding it for her, eyeing her expectantly. For the first time that she'd seen, he wore an elegant, woolen coat against the freezing cold outside.

With his back and shoulders perfectly straight, his eyes like granite on her, he was breathtaking.

Even the weather was restless today. Wind threw a rough gust of prickly snow into the side of her face. Her fingertips hurt from the cold as she put her hand on the rusty doorframe.

"Don't worry, Detective," Channing murmured. "There are no dragons or drug lords in there. And I'll be right by your side to protect you."

"Shut up," she replied and entered.

It smelled like machine oil, dust, and metal shavings. Her eyes had to adjust to the darkness after the blinding whiteness of the heavy snowfall outside. Channing came in after her, flicked a switch, and old, dirty LED lights running the length of the warehouse flooded the space with a harsh light. It was quiet here, only the buzzing of the lights came from above. Somewhere down the lines of long, metal shelves, a bulb flickered.

"What are those?" she said as she walked down the aisle between the rows of shelves filled with dirty cardboard boxes, bearings, chains, tools, and other metal parts. The shelves were marked with the names and numbers for those parts.

"Repair parts for ships," Channing said as he walked after her.

"And you said the building isn't used?"

"It's not."

"Doesn't it seem like a waste of precious real estate for such a successful businessman as yourself?" She brushed along the dusty side of one shelf and rubbed the dirt mixed with machine oil against her fingers. "Why do you come here then?"

He stopped walking behind her and, without looking at her, touched a box to align it against the edge of the shelf. "What if I'm hiding something here?"

"What are you hiding?"

He leaned against the shelf and met her gaze. "Can't tell you. The hiding wouldn't make sense, would it?"

"Channing..." she said with a warning.

He grinned. "My name sounds so good on your lips."

She sighed. "Stop flirting with me and answer my question."

"I can't help myself."

She didn't say anything. She'd made a mistake the first time she'd slept with him, then yesterday and again today, letting him get close. She was not acting like a police detective who could actually put him in prison.

"I come here to practice sword fighting," he said when she kept silent.

"Right," she said dubiously. "Wolves... Vikings with axes attacking you... Now you're sword fighting..."

"How do you think I keep in shape? I jog a little in the morning, but that's not enough. I work long hours at the port, so it makes sense to have a space here where I can exercise."

"Where?" she asked, looking around.

"In the back. Come, I'll show you."

He marched forward, too fast for her liking. She wanted to hang back and look around calmly, making note of details. But Channing was fast, and the hall was so big, she had a sense she could get lost in here. Distantly, she realized there was a place where the dirt on the concrete floor had been sort of swept away, and the concrete was shining, as if something had polished it.

"Here, come," Channing called. He'd already turned the corner of a shelf and she'd lost him.

She hurried and caught up with him in the maze of giant ship parts and wooden boxes.

They walked farther into the hall, and when they reached the back gates that Ella had seen when she'd inspected the building from the outside, a large space was revealed. Big enough for several trucks to fit in here.

"Here," he said as he started taking off his coat. "Can you hold this for a moment?"

She took his coat, and the sharp, earthy tang of his cologne mixed with the scent of his body made her swallow. She suppressed the urge to bury her face in the fabric and drink in his scent.

He went to one of the shelves and removed a sword. "There's no need to show me your moves with a sword," she said, laughing.

But as he walked towards her with the sword in his hand,

her laughter died. Suddenly, he wasn't a CEO anymore, not a modern man in an expensive tailor-made suit.

He was a warrior, ancient and primal. Just like the night of the storm, in the alley by the pub. His movement changed, his gait becoming more masculine, shoulders swaying from side to side. His face glowed, as if from an inner light, a strength she hadn't noticed before. And he held himself with the alertness of a predator.

A killer.

Her hand moved instinctively to the gun at her waist. He wasn't just playing or pretending. Those were the movements of someone who'd done this his whole life. The movements of a master.

She could easily imagine him in a different time, dressed as the men in the alley had been.

What if he was telling the truth? What if, by some miracle, he had traveled in time?

Her throat went dry.

She had seen him fight men who looked like real Vikings. And sword fighting was an unusual hobby for a billionaire...or anyone, really.

He laid the sword on his open palms and offered it to her. "I held my first sword when I was eight."

She studied the weapon. It was about thirty to thirty-five inches long, about two inches wide, and double-edged. She wondered if it was hard to swing with one hand. How much did it weigh? Three pounds? Four? The hilt was beautiful. The pommel was probably made of silver, with Norse symbols and ornate Viking patterns. The grip was made of some sort of antler and wrapped in silver cords. The blade looked new and unused and perfectly smooth.

Being a cop, she knew very well that a Massachusetts resident could own and carry a weapon on his property. Technically, the port was his property, so she let it slide.

An urge to reach out and take the sword in her hand tingled her fingers.

"It's beautiful," she said.

"Yes, it is," he said with a longing she didn't understand.

"Is this something you took with you when you time traveled?" She chuckled.

His jaw worked, an ache in his eyes making them dark as emeralds. "No. I had it made here."

He was just joking about time traveling. Surely, he was joking. "This whole Viking time travel thing is a metaphor, right?"

"It's easier for you to believe that, isn't it, Detective?"

Her eyes fell to the floor behind him and the spell broke. On the concrete were dirty tire tracks.

"And this is unused, you say?"

"Yes, these parts are old. Most modern ships use other parts and they're all stored closer to the wharfs, in building M08."

She looked at him for any sign of a lie, of nervousness. He put the sword back on a shelf and turned to her.

"Right," she said and gave him his coat back. "I'll need to look around."

With a frown, he accepted the coat. She knelt beside the tracks. The dirt was dry, so the tracks had been here for a while now. She took out her phone and took several pictures.

"What are you doing?" he asked.

"Taking pictures of the tire tracks."

He was looking at the tracks as though they were made of hot, smoldering lava.

"I have no idea what could have left those."

"Well, Mr. Hakonson," she said, disappointment weighing in her stomach like a boulder, "you claim this building hasn't been used, yet these tracks are evidence that it has. So either you're lying to me or someone's using the building without your knowledge."

He scowled at the tracks, looking around. "Without my knowledge?" he muttered.

She went over to the gates and studied the bolt. It showed evidence of use, with no rust apparent at the hinges. The floor was clean apart from the tracks. And the rows of shelves that stood next to the gate were empty, except for a couple of wooden boxes.

She walked towards one of them. "Do you train here alone?"

The surfaces weren't as dusty as the ones in the back, and there were patterns as if something had swept the dust in broad strokes. Crates? Boxes? Sacks or packs?

"Yes."

She leaned closer to the dust. No white powder that she could see. "Is this where you keep your sword?"

She went to the next shelf. Same.

"Only when I'm training. It's usually in my car."

"Why a real sword? Don't they use dummy swords in training? To not hurt anyone?"

By the third shelf, she stilled, spotting a small pile of dust... something white glistening there. She went into the inner pocket of her jacket and removed her evidence gathering kit.

Channing stood next to her. "I like the real thing. Makes me happy."

She put on the gloves and carefully slid a small portion of the dust into a one-ounce transparent evidence jar. She closed the lid and put it back into her jacket. She had the field drug test for cocaine in her car and she wanted to test the dust in peace because it would need some time.

She met his gaze.

"Do you think you'll find cocaine in there?" he asked, amused.

"I might," she said. "We'll see."

She moved to the next shelf, but her phone vibrated in her pocket. Still wearing gloves, she took out her phone.

Gloria.

Ella picked up. "Hi, Gloria."

"We're here."

"Okay. I'm coming."

"Everything okay?" Channing asked.

She nodded. She was sure if she had a proper look, she'd be able to discover more potential evidence.

"Is it okay if I look around later? Ted is here."

"Ted is here?" he said with a genuine smile, and was that a hint of relief? "Then let me show him around the port."

TWENTY-ONE

Ted waved enthusiastically from behind the security gate, and Channing waved back as he got out of his car.

Letting go of Gloria's hand, Ted ran towards the gate, gripping the bars with his mittened hands. "Can I look at the ships now, please, Ella?"

Ella climbed out of the car and walked towards him. "Ted, hon, there'll be a better time. I have to work, and I'm sure Mr. Hakonson is way too busy."

Channing's heart melted at the sight of the hopeful boy. Bryan sat inside the car, scowling at everyone. Gloria kissed Ted's head in his knitted hat. "Now, be a good boy. Thanks, Ella, hon!"

Ted nodded. "I always am, Mom."

Gloria glanced back at the road behind the car. "Now, Ella. Perhaps it's not a bad idea that you two stay at the port for a while."

Ella frowned. "What? Why?"

Gloria sighed. "Some streets are completely blocked by the

hunger demonstration. The storm caused major food delays. There are more and more hungry people on the streets."

"But how are you going to get to the hospital then? Mass Gen is right in the heart of the city."

"We'll be fine. Your dad still knows the best routes. And we really can't miss this appointment."

"Let me take him then, and you stay with Ted."

"No, it's fine." She leaned closer to Ella. "Your dad is more likely to listen to me than to you."

Channing glanced again at Bryan, who glowered at him. Didn't matter. He had seen the glimpse of hope when Ella got the call from Gloria. He'd give anything to keep that hope up for her. Half a million was nothing.

Ella nodded and gestured for Ted to come to this side of the gate. Gloria kissed Ella, turned, and hurried towards the car.

As Ted and Ella walked back to Channing, he saw her worry. Gloria was right, they'd be safe here in the port until the protests died out. Plus he wasn't ready for Ella to leave yet, and he genuinely liked her brother.

Channing clapped Ted on the shoulder. "So, buddy, ready to see some ships?"

Ted looked at the tops of the container ships jutting up from behind the warehouses and the line of containers stacked on top of one another. He nodded, wide-eyed.

"Then let's go."

Channing exchanged a glance with Ella. When they climbed back into his car and he drove down the lane, Ella, who sat in the passenger seat, leaned closer to him. "Thanks for doing this. I know we're interrupting your day."

He smiled at her. He could drive Ted and her around all day. Strangely, an image flooded his heart—them as a suburban couple, taking their kid to the zoo, hands intertwined, exchanging smiles of happiness.

For the first time ever, he thought of his future with a woman. And that future wasn't in the ninth century.

It was here.

Taking a deep breath to chase the feeling, as heavy as rock, from his chest, he looked straight at the road in front of him. "It's my pleasure, Detective. I meant it. Ted is a great kid, and I have no one to share my passion for ships with."

He glanced into the mirror at Ted, who was practically plastered against the window. He exhaled slowly, fighting the ache in his heart as he thought of his own brother, remembering when their father had taken them to trade with the Baltic tribes. John'd watched the flat, sandy coastline with eyes as wide as moons, glistening with the spirit of adventure and exploration.

"Ships are freedom," Channing said. "The sea is life. That's why I love everything that's connected with the ocean."

He felt Ella's gaze on him, like warm tingling on his face. "Who are you?" she whispered. "Who are you, really?"

His face softened. "Just a lost man looking for a way back home."

She blinked, her eyes watering. Their eyes locked—for an eternity, and in that moment, there was a promise of everything. Of a future that was possible. And a past that didn't exist.

"Isn't this nice?" he said.

What he meant was, right now, he wasn't a suspect, a CEO, and a billionaire. And she wasn't a police detective who was on his tail. At the end of the day, he was just a man. And she was the most beautiful woman in the world.

She nodded. "It is."

As they drove, Channing was pointing at the ships that were docked by the container cranes and telling Ted their weight, where they came from, and how many containers they were carrying. He told him how they were built and that a port like Boston's had to provide an opportunity for the ships to have maintenance. He told about the history of ships, and that while now ships were built from fiberglass and metal, the first ships in history were made of wood.

At the very end of the quay, they stopped and climbed out. "There." Channing pointed at a ship that was navigated by a tugboat. "See that small boat?"

Ted nodded.

"That's a tugboat. Even though it's so small, that boat helps the giant ships arrive safely to the port."

"Really?"

"Yeah," said Channing, exchanging a smile with Ella, who was beaming delightedly at her brother. "Sometimes a big guy would sink without a small one. Sometimes that's what's needed, someone small."

Ted nodded, staring at the ship that was arriving slowly. "What's the name?"

Channing narrowed his eyes. The container ship was flying a Norwegian flag. As it came closer, he stopped breathing, his blood freezing.

"*Naglfar*," he muttered.

"What does it carry?" Ted asked.

A nuclear reactor...

Suddenly, all the warmth, the sense of normality, and every hopeful thought evaporated from his body.

What was it doing here? It was too early.

"Um. It's just a container ship, buddy. All sorts of goods. Oil, probably, if it's from Norway. They excavate oil from the North Sea."

Ted's mouth made a perfect O. "Come on," said Channing. "Let's look at other ships."

"Where is Norway?" asked Ted as though he hadn't heard Channing.

"It's in Europe," said Ella.

It's where I was born.

"Come on," said Channing. "Let's look at something else."

He knew he sounded worried, and it didn't escape Ella's notice. She frowned at him and then at the ship. "I want to look at oil from Norway," said Ted stubbornly.

Fuck.

"You know what?" said Ella. "Me, too."

Traitor...

She narrowed her eyes at Channing and then kept watch on the ship that had Channing's destiny—and a lifetime prison sentence—on board.

About half an hour passed, and the ship was docking at the wharf. It was so close, Channing could see every indent in the sea-salt-caked stern. Ted eyed it up and down like it was a miracle that had arrived at his feet. Then he frowned and looked closely at the hull, right next to the seam in the metal. "Channing, what is this? Is it a mussel?"

As Channing looked closer, horror froze his bones like nitrogen. Right in the metal, was...

"It's a human fingernail," said Ella, astonished.

How could it be there? It was just like in the prophecy about Ragnarök.

Naglfar, the ship of fingernails, will sail with the people of Hel, and at the helm will stand Loki, the god of mischief.

Although Channing couldn't see Loki himself, or anyone from the land of the dead, a chill ran through him. More and more weird shit was going on in the world...and it was all pointing towards Ragnarök. And if they were really experiencing the mythical *Fimbulwinter*, which would hold the planet in its icy grip for three years, the end of the world was inevitable.

Would his nuclear reactor be the final element needed to

bring on Ragnarök through some sort of environmental disaster? Would using the time machine destroy everything?

If so, should he stop his project? Should he abandon his attempt to go back to the ninth century? Should he let his family die?

No. Who was to say that this really was Ragnarök? The thought of letting his family die was soul-wrenching. He couldn't live with himself if he didn't try.

A noise came from behind him, and Channing looked back. A black SUV stopped behind his car, and one of the windows rolled down. Somewhere down the road, behind the SUV, Channing saw something that made him want to rub his eyes.

A crowd.

People marched down the street that led from the central gate to the wharf.

Ella put her hands on Ted's shoulders. "Channing..." Ella said, a warning in her voice.

Channing's eyes didn't leave the black SUV. "Wait here. Stay with Ted."

He strode towards the SUV and in the dark depths of the cabin, he saw Leo Esposito. He doubted Ella could see him from that distance.

Channing put his hands on the door where the window was open. "What the fuck is this? I was told *Naglfar* would arrive in three days."

Leo Esposito cocked his head. "Yes, it was supposed to."

"So why is it here now?"

"Why aren't you happy? Usually, people get angry when things are delayed. You got your delivery early. Rejoice."

"The logistics of this are fucked up," Channing said through gritted teeth.

Leo looked past him at Ella. "You mean, because you have a beautiful police detective and her brother with you today?"

Odin's arse, how did he know?

"Exactly. You know the police discovered one of your containers."

"Yes. And they will discover more. Have you thought about my proposal?"

"No."

"No, you haven't, or no, you're not going to work with me?"

Channing just needed to hold him off for a few more days. "I haven't thought about it."

"Well, until you do, I think this argument might persuade you." Leo looked through his other window at the approaching crowd. "Rumors were spread among the protestors that there was plenty of food delivered to the port despite the storm."

Channing's face fell. "What?"

"Hungry people are a dangerous force, Mr. Hakonson. I hope you know that this is just one of the ways I can be persuasive. You have three more days to give me your answer."

The window rolled up, and the car drove off, taking another route.

Part of the crowd turned towards one of the warehouses, and Channing heard shouts of pain. Suddenly, it was as though a switch had been flicked, and the crowd roared. The protestors ran inside the warehouse. Many of them had sticks, and Channing even saw guns glinting.

"Get in the car!" he yelled without turning. "Both of you." When nothing happened, he looked back over his shoulder. "Now, Ella!"

Ted's eyes were round and terrified. Ella ushered him towards the car. As Ted climbed in, Channing noticed how shaken the poor boy was, pale, his lower lip trembling.

The sounds of gunshots and more yells came from the warehouse.

"In the car!" yelled Channing to Ella as he climbed into the driver's seat. She got into the passenger seat, and he drove with a screech of tires against the asphalt.

"Ted," said Ella, "it's going to be okay. You know I'm a police officer and I have a gun to protect you, right?"

"Yes."

"Okay. Good. I'm going to take the gun out now, but it's only for our protection, all right? Everything is going to be okay."

Ted nodded, his lower lip still shaking.

Ella went to her holster. "Good." She took out her gun and held it on her lap.

As they drove past the warehouses, the metal roofs glistening in the blinding sun, Ella looked at him. "Who was that in the car?"

Maneuvering onto the second road that ran along the port, Channing cursed. The road was filled with a crowd, also. There were only two roads from here to the administration building. Gunshots were fired ahead of them, and the crowd spilled into the warehouse. They must have found food because some of them were coming out of the buildings with crates, and others grabbed the crates and were trying to pull them from their hands.

Brothers killing brothers... The wolf age... The hunger age...

"Doesn't matter who was in the car," Channing growled through gritted teeth. "What matters is how we get out of here."

"Just go," said Ella.

He nodded and accelerated the car. The most important thing now was that the boy in the back seat and the woman sitting by his side came out of this alive. As he drove closer to the crowd, he saw his employees fighting with the rioters. Goddamn it. He didn't care about the financial loss. But he did care about the lives of the people he was responsible for. The rioters could take all the food for all he cared.

The deliveries of avocados, bananas, rice, and other fruits and vegetables had become more and more infrequent, but some were still delivered.

As they drove closer to the crowd, people looked at the car. Though some faces had red, weathered skin, other people were dressed in regular winter clothes: padded jackets, coats, hats. Most didn't even look homeless. They were just regular people, but the desperation, the edge of despair that was on their faces —that told him more than anything else. Perhaps he wasn't the only one who knew none of this would end well.

Channing rolled down his window. "Keep your gun down," he told Ella.

He had to stop the car because the crowd wasn't moving. Many were fighting for food, while others were gnawing at unripe, hard-as-rocks avocados right there.

"What are you doing?" Ella whispered.

Channing leaned from his window. "Hey, guys! Richard-son!" One of the workers who was holding a crate away from one of the protestors looked up and met his eyes. "Don't fight them, give them anything they want."

Richardson frowned. "But Mr. Hakonson..."

"Don't worry, none of you will be in trouble. Just let them take the food."

Richardson nodded and handed the woman the crate.

But before Channing could roll up his window, one of the men who stood next to the car frowned at him. "Hakonson? You're the port owner, aren't you?"

Something about that tone, the edge of malice, made Channing's skin chill. "Yes," he said. "Just let us pass."

"Hey," the man cried out to the crowd. "This is one of them. The one-percenters. The rich ones."

The crowd stilled, and Channing had a strange, nightmarish feeling that they all looked at him at once.

What could he say to that? Yes, he was one of the rich ones. And they clearly blamed him for their hardships. Was he responsible?

You are the reason for Ragnarök, he remembered Eirik's words.

Was the völva right? What if his presence in the Viking Age had been a mistake? He was trying to bend magic to his needs by using science and making his own destiny. Was that the reason for the end of everything?

His gut churned as the next thought came... Would his death save the world?

No, that couldn't be right... He refused to believe that.

Channing's hand curled around the wheel. "Let us pass. I don't want anyone to get hurt."

"You motherfucker," said the man slowly. "It's you, isn't it? It's all because of you. The climate change. The hunger. The rich get richer. The poor get poorer." The man's weathered face wrinkled into a grimace of anger. "You will pay."

He jumped onto the car and opened the door. Channing pressed the button to lock it but was too late, and the door swung open. The crowd roared, and hands and arms reached for Channing, grabbed him, and pulled. Ted shrieked in a shrill, siren-like tone.

"Let him go!" yelled Ella, tugging Channing back into the car. "Let him go!"

Channing was kicking, pushing back, hitting faces, shoulders, arms, but they were too strong. There were too many of them. They hauled him out, and a fist hit him in the face. Pain exploded through his skull, but he didn't stagger back. He stood his ground and called on all the battle rage the gods have ever given him, and roared.

The crowd stopped for a moment, staring at him with wild, astonished eyes.

"You want to fight me?" Channing cried. "One-on-one is a fair fight, man-to-man. This is madness." In the car, Ella was staring at him with eyes as round as saucers. He knew she wanted to help, but she had her brother to think about, and Ted was still producing the high-pitched, shrill cry. The boy needed her. "Ella, drive!"

"Well, fuck you!" cried one of the men, a big, sturdy guy with a gray face and the black teeth of a crack addict.

He threw the crate he was holding to the frozen asphalt. The wood exploded in splinters and planks, avocados rolling into snow. He grabbed one of the planks with two nails still sticking out of it. Other men followed his example and took their own planks.

"You fucked us," said the first man. "Now it's payday, you rich cocksucker."

Channing clenched his fists, ready to fight. "Drive, Ella! Go!"

Right before the first man hauled his hands back with the stick for a hard blow, Channing saw within his peripheral vision that Ella had climbed into the driver's seat and put her hands on the wheel. Her phone was in her other hand, but her worried, wild eyes were on him. She was probably calling for backup. And sooner or later, the port police and the customs guys would surely arrive, too. They must be on the way. He only needed to hold on for a few moments.

The plank with the nails flew by his face as the man swung it. He ducked and it missed, but something blunt hit him in the kidney, and all the breath left his body. As the third plank swung, he hit back, knocking the man's arm away. He lost the plank, and Channing grabbed it in midair.

He deflected the next blow, but the roar of the crowd

around him intensified. More people came for him, hating that the man they blamed for their misfortunes was fighting back.

A blow landed on the back of his head, sinking the world into a white fog of pain for a moment. Blinded, he swung the plank in a wide, furious, horizontal arc, hitting someone. A groan of pain came from the man, and then blows rained down on him like hail.

He kept fighting, but he knew he couldn't win. He could only stall them.

Then came a blow so hard, he heard a crack of bone. Or maybe it was a gunshot.

He didn't know. The world shifted and he fell. The icy road under his face was a welcome pillow as the roar of the crowd disappeared and everything sank into a loud, wild ringing in his ears.

And then there was nothing.

TWENTY-TWO

Ella saw Channing fall and get swallowed by the crowd. Despite her training and years on the job, terror rooted her to the spot.

She knew how dangerous an angry mob could be, how out of control normally rational people could become. And Channing was unarmed and at their mercy.

Ted's shrill cry elevated to a new pitch behind her.

It felt like things were escalating all around her...and across the globe. Could the end of the world truly be coming? And if Channing was somehow the cause, would letting him die save them all?

The thought made her sick, sour acid rising in her stomach. The crowd roared, pushing against one another, trying to get to him.

Do something!

She remembered the day her father got shot. How Ella had thought that was it. Now she'd be an orphan. How pain had crushed her within—loneliness, abandonment.

She'd almost lost him then.

She could lose Channing now.

Reality stopped. Froze like a movie set on pause. Ted's shrill cry died down. She turned around to look at him—his mouth was open, hands pressed to his ears, nose wrinkled in the grimace of an unending yell.

The sounds of the crowd became a muffled noise, as if she were underwater. She got out of the car, breathing hard. Her gun was in her hand. How could she have just stopped time? Was she dreaming?

No. This was real. Frighteningly real.

She couldn't see Channing because of the crowd, but she knew he must be there, in what looked like a small funnel where they surrounded him and were probably giving him a good beating.

She had to help. She had to save him. She'd think about this weird time-stopping thing later. She raised her hand straight up in the air and fired her gun.

Time restarted as the explosion burst through the air. Then, everything went still. Ted stopped screaming. The crowd froze, then turned to her. Her stomach dropped, and her feet turned to lead. This must be how an ant felt before the unstoppable force of a human boot landed on it.

How could she stop them alone? She wouldn't shoot into the crowd.

But then, in that dead silence, the distant howl of a wolf came. Then yapping mixed with growls approached, closer and closer.

The wolves. Dozens of them—maybe a hundred—emerged from the corner of a warehouse in a sea of gray and brown fur. Fangs flashed at they ripped into people's hands, necks, legs... The growls of deadly predators and screams of terrified people chilled her blood.

Ella went cold and numb. The scene from her mother's embroidery was unfolding before her eyes.

Shots were fired through the crowd, followed by pained animal yelps and human cries.

She aimed her gun at the animals, but in the wild entanglement of man and beast, she couldn't know where she was firing and which she would hit.

Sirens sounded, closer and closer. Channing forgotten, the crowd ran.

Ella's heart pounded in relief as port police, ambulances, and Boston Police were arriving. Some people in the crowd were stopped, many arrested.

The wolves didn't attack the officers, as though they knew these people wouldn't harm Channing. As the crowd dissolved, they surrounded Channing just like they had with the Vikings, licking his wounds, staring at humans wearing uniform with a cool warning.

Ella carefully approached them, her hands shaking under their wary gazes. They did nothing to her. They just took off like a grayish-brown wind and disappeared behind the warehouses.

TWELVE HOURS LATER, Channing lay unconscious from the sedative the ER doctor had given him. His eyes were closed, the long, dark, curly eyelashes casting small shadows from the harsh hospital lights. His chest rose and fell evenly, but he was as pale as death. His forehead was misted with sweat, the hospital gown with a blue geometric pattern looked odd on him. His shoulder was bandaged and, she guessed, the wound on his side, too. Something was so terribly wrong about seeing a man like Channing Hakonson—the image of masculine strength and power—in a hospital bed, unconscious. Seeing him so helpless and vulnerable made Ella's gut turn.

Please, live...

Silly, of course he was going to live. The doctor had told her so. He'd lost a lot of blood, but the scans showed that luckily the nails hadn't gone in deep enough to damage any organs. They'd managed to stitch his puncture wounds, so he was out of danger.

Ella's hand itched to touch him. If he were conscious, she'd have never done anything like this, but since he was out cold, he'd never know.

Hand shaking, she reached out and brushed a lock of dark, sweat-misted hair from Channing's forehead. His skin was smooth, and he smelled like himself—the manly, earthy tang mixed with some shampoo or body wash that made her think of long sea journeys and tall mountains with untouched forests, and air as crisp as ice.

She studied the pale, uneven brown heart-shaped birthmark on his left temple and wondered if he'd gotten it from his mother or his father. What had happened to his father, whose name didn't appear on his birth certificate? If Channing was truly a Viking who had traveled in time—an idea she was feeling more open to after seeming to have stopped time herself more than once—he must miss his family terribly.

She may lose her father, too.

Ella hadn't been in the hospital since her dad had been shot. The smell of Mass Gen tickled her nostrils, spiking her anxiety on yet another level. Following the ambulances, she'd come to the hospital with Ted, where she'd met Gloria and Dad and they took him home.

One piece of good news was that Dad's doctor said they wanted to operate in a couple of days, after which Dad would get radiation and a new chemotherapy that was experimental but showed high promise.

No one had come for Channing. No friends or relatives. No one cared if he lived or died. And she just couldn't leave him. She was no one to him—just a woman he'd slept with a couple of times, a woman who was trying to find a way to get him behind bars.

Ricardo had come by and she'd given him the plate number of the black SUV. Back in the station, he'd looked it up and said it was registered in the name of a flower delivery company and that there was nothing suspicious about it, not on the surface. He'd also picked up the drug sample and taken it to the lab, and now they were waiting for the results.

She knew the lab might find cocaine in the sample, that she should keep her distance from an already compromised suspect. But she couldn't leave Channing's side.

What had happened back there? she wondered. Why hadn't she used her gun sooner?

If she had, Channing wouldn't be in the hospital, wounded.

The world was going insane. She must have gone insane. People attacking one another, raiding a seaport...trying to kill Channing, who had basically told them to go ahead and take any food they wanted.

Winter had hit the whole globe so hard that both people and animals had a shortage of food. Wild animals were coming into cities, looking for warmth and food—that might explain the wolves. Or maybe, like rats on a sinking ship, they sensed they were about to die and were fleeing, only there was no escape.

The thought unsettled Ella.

She brushed her knuckles against Channing's cheek, the stubble rough against her skin. The sensation brought the memory of their kiss—the way his tongue had brushed against hers, the way his stubble had burned her lips, the way she'd melted, turning into warm honey in his arms.

He opened his eyes. They were clouded with drowsiness, but they were right on her.

Shock and embarrassment washed over her in a cold wave, but she was unable to move, mesmerized. No one and nothing existed around them. The ticking of the clock slowed, and there was so much warmth and love and relief in his eyes, she lost her ability to breathe.

"This feels nice..." he whispered.

She snatched her hand back from his face as though he was red-hot.

"Ella..." he croaked.

Her cheeks were on fire. "Are you okay?" she said, rubbing her hand. It felt numb and cold without the warmth of his skin.

"Já," he said. It meant *yes*. He spoke Old Norse, she knew instinctively. Again, she could understand it—how? "I'm fine."

He propped himself up with his arms and winced.

"Shall I call the nurse?"

"No."

"Are you sure?"

"I'm fine. Why are you here?"

She cleared her throat and turned away for a moment, biting her lip. She'd had to stay with him to fill out the information in the incident report. But, if she was honest, that wasn't the only reason she'd stayed. She just couldn't leave him alone like that.

"I need to fill out the police report. You don't have anyone in your emergency contact info. Can I call someone for you?"

"There's no one to call," he said. "When can I get out of here?"

He was cold and rough and distant yet again. The warmth

and light that they'd shared when he'd opened his eyes was gone.

"Let me call the nurse," she said and walked out of his room. How could he have no one to take care of him? What kind of life was he leading? Why was he so lonely?

The answer fit with his insane explanation.

Time travel. She shook her head, reminding herself that there were plenty of people who lived alone and had solitary lives.

She found the nurse, who came to Channing's bed with a tray of Jell-O and some water and updated him, saying that they just needed to keep him in the hospital for a day or so. He needed antibiotics and an IV. He'd lost some blood, but the wounds from the nails were not life-threatening.

"I'm fine," he growled. "I don't have time to stay here. I'd like to be discharged."

The nurse frowned. "No, this is really—"

"I can get discharged against your recommendation, can't I?" he said.

"Of course, but sir—"

"Start the paperwork, please."

"Let me call the doctor first. Maybe she can explain better." She left with a frown.

"You're really not okay, buddy," said Ella, her arms crossed over her chest.

He opened his Jell-O and took a spoonful. "Don't worry about me."

"Where do you need to go in such a hurry, anyway?"

"Did you see what happened in the port? Our security has been breached. I need to see the damage, and I can't do that in a hospital. Plus, my wounds aren't that bad."

Suddenly, she was angry at him. Another stubborn man who was denying medical help. She'd just managed to convince her dad to accept the treatment that may save his life or at least allow him to live longer.

"I just don't get you men," she said. "What is so bad about getting help?"

He frowned at her. "We men just think there's too much fuss about nothing."

"Nothing?" She scoffed and went to sit on the chair by his bed. "My dad is dying of cancer."

He swallowed his Jell-O and took another spoonful, wincing like it tasted bitter. "Yes. You told me."

"An anonymous donation was made that covers his medical bills. You don't know anything about that?"

"No."

She leaned back in the chair. "And what if I suggested you made that donation?"

"What if I did?"

"Do you realize the consequences if this gets out?"

"I'm just glad your dad gets treatment."

She shook her head and let out a long sigh. She eyed him. He was so stern and still pale, and though he was managing to eat the Jell-O, she could see that his hands were shaking. And even so pale and so weak, he was as handsome as a Norse god.

"Can I ask you something?" she said, leaning over the bed on her elbows. "And I want you to be real with me. No lies. Nothing. So, say you were born in another time. And the Norns did bring you here. What are you doing? You want something, don't you?"

He studied her with a strange longing. "Not everyone is lucky enough to have their family alive," he said with a surprising softness. "I read in an old manuscript that my family died in a horrific fire. I have to return to their time and save them."

"With a time machine?"

He exhaled a long breath. He didn't reply for a while, as if gathering his thoughts. Something dark flashed through his eyes, and when he met her gaze, a stony wall had been erected. "I have no magical abilities. I use science instead."

She sighed and shook her head. "That I actually can believe."

He ate another spoon of Jell-O. "Really?"

"Yeah. I can imagine there are mad scientists around the world who're trying to do the same. Doesn't mean it can be done."

He put the empty Jell-O cup on the side table. "Unfortunately, that is true."

"But if you were conceived in this century, your father must be from here."

He stilled. All life left his expression, as though a strong gust of wind had extinguished a candle.

"What? Do you know who he is?"

He nodded. "My mother didn't want anything to do with the man who fathered me. Neither did I."

Ella swallowed. There was something about this she could relate to. Something in his voice, the pain she knew, too.

"Why?" she asked.

He fingered the plastic spoon in his hand. "Because he raped her. That is how I came to exist."

She had met enough rape victims during her first five years as a street cop to know how bad it was for them. She'd also met children of those rape victims—children who, unfortunately, witnessed the abuse in their own homes. Her heart broke every time she had to interview them, every time she had to hear those stories.

And she'd heard enough of them to know that wounds like that were hard to heal.

"I'm sorry," she said.

He chuckled. "Yes. Well. Some things can't be changed, no matter how much you want them to."

She nodded. "Yes, that's true."

She thought of her own mother. Of the million ways she could try to be better, to change herself so that her mother would love her and stay. But, like Channing had said, that wasn't possible.

"I know." She looked at her hands and let out a long breath to release a painful knot that had gathered in her chest.

It was hard to talk about, needles stabbing her lungs as she tried to get the words out. It was her dark secret, the pain she'd held in and didn't let out even for her father.

It was like a big, old, ugly painting hanging on the wall that you want to throw away but can't. And so you try to ignore it, but it's just there, it's always there, tainting the room no matter where you look.

"Are you thinking about your mother?" he asked.

She looked up at him. There was sadness in his eyes, and also something else—pain. Regret. Tenderness.

She nodded.

"She was an idiot to let you go, Ella. But you should know one thing. And I'm saying this with your best interests in mind."

His eyes darkened and shone with intensity.

"Once my time machine works, I will be gone. So no matter how much I can't get enough of you, stay away from me. I'm not the right man for you."

She blinked at the sudden hurt that those words caused her. But before she could say anything, her phone vibrated. Glad for a distraction, she picked up without looking at the caller ID.

"O'Connor," she barked.

"This is Peterson from the lab. We got your results back.

There was cocaine in the dust. One of the purest we've ever seen."

Her fingers clenched around the phone. Channing had lied. Maybe it was all a lie. She held him in her gaze as her chest exploded with the shattered pieces of the illusion he had created.

"Thanks." She hung up.

Logically, she had known this was a possibility. The cop in her was hunting for evidence, looking for a reason to arrest him or anyone responsible for the trafficking.

But her heart...her stupid, stupid heart didn't believe she could have fallen for a criminal and a liar.

The things she'd told him... The things he'd told her... The things they'd done together... Yes, she had hoped he wouldn't turn out to be a criminal.

But he had. The evidence didn't lie.

And just like when she was four years old and her mother betrayed her, turning her world into a lonely and dark place.

So had Channing Hakonson.

The lengths he'd gone to distract her from the investigation —the story about time travel, Vikings, and the end of the world...

He'd made her feel like the biggest fool now.

She had fallen for a criminal and a liar and risked everything for him.

He frowned. "What?"

"I hope you have a lawyer, Mr. Hakonson." Not feeling her legs, she stood up. "There were cocaine traces in Mo5. I'm getting a search warrant immediately. It seems you're not who I thought you were. You can find your own way home."

TWENTY-THREE

"The police are here," yelled Peter van Beek over the phone. "They have a search warrant."

Slowly standing up from his bed, Channing growled. "Did you manage to install the package or not?"

Channing had had a conversation with Peter two days ago, after he'd discharged himself from the hospital. Channing had promised van Beek to get his daughter into Boston University where Channing was a guest lecturer for Old Norse in exchange for arranging the transportation and installation of the reactor off the books.

"For fuck's sake, it's still in the ship. I'm telling you, you'd better get here. You'd better make sure they discover *nothing*. Or it's both our careers and life in prison on the line!"

"On my way."

Channing hung up, set his laptop on his bed, wincing from pain. He was still a little woozy from the blood loss and ached from the bruises and the puncture wounds. Yes, he had a slight concussion, but it was just a little headache. He was taking the iron pills and the antibiotics, he'd be fine.

The physical pain was nothing compared to the excruciating ache inside his chest that had torn him apart when he'd seen the look on Ella's face after that call.

What did it matter if he was going to leave this century, anyway? He'd known from the beginning that they weren't meant to be together. He wasn't meant to be with anyone.

Anyone but her, whispered his heart. *That's why you're feeling like a bomb has torn you apart.*

Didn't matter, he told himself again as he undid the buttons on his pj's.

The line between the law and the criminal world had never been thinner. His biological father was long dead, and yet he still carried the burden of his legacy.

A legacy that had alienated Ella, the only woman who made warmth spread in his chest. She'd shared something very intimate with him, and she was the one person who knew the whole truth about him.

He was falling in love with her. But the irony was, now that he'd found her, he was bound to disappear from this time.

During the past day, he'd contacted his lawyer, just as she'd suggested, and prepared a will. Upon his disappearance or death, he was giving all his wealth to a trust fund for her and her family. Her mortgage would be paid and Bryan's medical bills would all be taken care of.

He also wrote a letter explaining that he was leaving the States forever and wanted to live alone in the wilderness, tired of the pressures of the business world. He was going on a spiritual journey and didn't want to be found.

He had to make sure no one would be suspicious that someone had murdered or kidnapped him, especially not Ella.

When he was ready, he gave in and took the painkillers, then called the cab, still unable to drive. As the taxi was approaching the port, he saw a dozen cars lined up before the gate. Channing paid and got out, moving much easier now that the painkillers had kicked in.

He walked down the line, glowering at the cops who stood around talking. In front, at the gate, Ella was speaking to the guard, showing him a paper.

"Detective O'Connor," Channing called, and she turned her head to him. Ricardo Sanchez stood next to her, scowling. "Congratulations, you got your warrant."

Their eyes locked, hers glaring. "Yes. We were just about to drive in."

Channing nodded to the guard, who went back into his booth and lifted the barrier.

"Any chance I could ride with you?" Channing said. "I came by cab."

She scanned him up and down, concern flashing across her face for a moment. "Should you even be out of bed?"

Ricardo Sanchez threw a sharp glance at her, then at Channing.

Damn it. She didn't need anyone to know about their affair. He surely wasn't going to let anyone know, but she should be careful, too.

Channing stood straighter. "I'm fine."

The crease between her eyebrows didn't soften. "Get in."

He climbed into Ella's Taurus, noting that the bumper had been recently repaired and still needed paint. When they were driving, silence hung in the car. Channing caught Ricardo's hard stare at him in the mirror. Ella was at the wheel, her eyes pointedly on the road in front of her. Several of the port's warehouse buildings had needed to be closed to repair the damage done by the riot. There was a huge insurance mess to deal with. And because a lot of produce had been damaged or stolen, the supply chain to the supermarkets had been interrupted, putting the city in an even worse food shortage.

Which led to more unrest.

Added to that, the temperature had grown even colder.

Ella said, "We start at Mo5."

Channing chuckled. "Sure. I want to see your face when you find nothing."

The lab was hidden well enough, he told himself. He was fine.

Ricardo cleared his throat. "You realize we will testify to everything you're saying?"

"Then it's good I have no drugs to hide."

Ella tapped on the wheel with her thumb. "Another team is going into your office and will be searching there," she said without looking at him.

Silence hung in the car as they parked by building Mo5. Both cops had "we'll see" expressions on their faces.

Snowdrifts surrounded the perimeter of the parking area, brilliant white against the gray sky. Channing hated to see Ella so distant, so cold after he'd seen her at her happiest and most vulnerable.

As the rest of the police cars were arriving, Channing got out and looked at the line of ships docked by the blue unloading cranes. The one at the very end of the port was *Naglfar*, giant and black, looming over the port like a mountain. A mountain in the belly of which was Channing's way to another world.

Channing had read yesterday that someone had lost their fingers during its construction, and the fingernails and parts of fingers had landed in the molten metal and were never retrieved. Apparently, that was how the ship had gotten its name.

According to the article, which referred to Ragnarök, the man had died soon after in another unconnected accident. The author was wondering if this ship would somehow cause

Ragnarök, but she was clearly joking and just found the coincidence interesting.

If she only knew...

Channing opened the door to the building and let the police pour inside. Thirty or so police men and women swept past him. They strung yellow caution tape around the building, and men and women with bags full of what was probably equipment to gather forensic evidence spilled all over the perimeter.

Inside Mo5, Channing stood in the corner watching them turn over boxes, shift shelves, and scrub dust into evidence kits.

Based on Ella's findings, the Mafia was clearly using Mo5 without his knowledge. How could he have missed it? Had they operated at night? That was the only time he wasn't at the port.

There must be someone among his employees they were working with. Who?

If he were staying in this century, he'd get to the bottom of this right away. But he was leaving. Odin help him, he was leaving. If he could avoid being arrested or being killed by the Mafia—his grandfather was expecting his answer today.

He rubbed his chin. "Fuck this," he muttered. His gut was churning. Yesterday, he had told Munchie and Georgina to stay away from the lab until the police left them alone. How long would it take? He was so close to the end—they only needed to install the reactor.

Days? Weeks? Months?

If not for the police threat and his grandfather, he wouldn't mind the long wait. It would let him stay with Ella longer.

In fact, he didn't want to leave her at all. The thought of living in a world where she didn't exist made him want to tear his chest open and howl at the moon like a goddamn wolf.

He noticed a cop go up to shelf number three in row thirteen, where the entrance into the basement was. He moved the crates and looked inside, then touched the fake part of the shelf behind which the keypad was hidden. Channing went completely still, fighting to breathe. The cop was so close to discovering the secret entrance. If he moved the cover, he'd find it...

"Channing Hakonson!" called Ella's voice behind him. He turned. Ella with several other cops marched towards him. Her face was expressionless...

"You're under arrest for drug trafficking and possession of illegal substances. You have the right to remain silent. Anything you say can and will be used against you in a court of law..."

He stopped hearing, the pulse in his ears drumming so hard everything else was muffled. Ella grabbed his hands and twisted them at his back, the jolt of electricity between them still as strong and exhilarating as ever, despite the cold, unforgiving handcuffs that bit into his wrists and closed with a soft metallic clank.

As he turned to her, there wasn't a trace of triumph in her eyes. Or coldness. Or disgust.

Only the hurt of someone who had just been betrayed.

TWENTY-FOUR

"Ready to go in?" asked Ricardo.

Ella was ready, all right. There he was, through the two-way mirror, sitting in the interrogation room...

The man who'd deeply disappointed her. Who'd hurt her. The hurt that she remembered from her mother's leaving.

He hadn't left her, and even if he had, what was there to be disappointed about?

And yet...

And yet he was a drug trafficker, after all. They'd found a bag of cocaine hidden in a safe behind the artwork that had witnessed her coming on his desk.

That had witnessed her falling for a criminal. A fucking drug trafficker.

He'd told her ridiculous lies about time traveling and being a Viking... And she had allowed herself—even for a moment—to believe that it might be true. How could she be so clueless?

Would he betray her again? Would he use their affair to get out of this? Or would he keep his promise to her?

Wilson turned to her. "Ella?"

His face was red and stony, jaw muscles flexing under the fat flesh. His skin glistened in the blue light of the computer monitors.

She picked up the file. "Ready."

Wilson jabbed a sausage finger at her. "Don't fuck this up. You get him. This is your chance, O'Connor."

With her gut twisting, she nodded. There was really no great outcome in this scenario. Either she would get a confession out of him and put the man she was falling for in prison. Or he'd use her weakness—her affair with him—and stab her in the back.

In which case, she'd get fired and lose everything.

All because of him. The traitor.

No, she shouldn't be angry with Channing Hakonson, she thought as Ricardo and she walked out to the gray corridor.

As she swung the door to the interrogation room open, she decided the only person she really should be angry at was herself. She could have stopped him. She should have said no.

She should have never fallen under his charms.

Her eyes met Channing's as she entered the small, concrete-walled room illuminated by harsh LED lights.

The handsome bastard looked like shit, sitting at the single table next to his lawyer. Channing's face had a grayish undertone with dark circles under his green eyes. Sweat misted his forehead and his mouth was tight in a grimace...

A grimace of pain, she recognized.

As she sat across the table from him, she realized he'd spent around twelve hours here. Regret over causing him pain and discomfort stabbed at her, but she shook it away. He deserved every bit of pain he got if he was providing Boston with illegal drugs.

Channing's lawyer was a black woman in her forties with bright-red hair. She had a soft, friendly expression as though they were gathered for high tea, and not because of a criminal investigation.

The lawyer nodded. "Hello. I'm Giana Kilpatrick, Mr. Hakonson's lawyer."

Ella opened her folder. "Hello," she said. Ricardo echoed her.

The LED lights buzzed above their heads, but her heart beat louder in her temples. There were so many things she wanted to tell him. She wanted to hit him. To kick herself in the butt for thinking of him so much, for dreaming about him, for falling for the wrong man.

And he did warn her. He did say he was not the right man for her. This was no doubt what he'd meant. A drug-smuggling Robin Hood who gave his drug money to charity and had almost certainly funded her dad's treatment.

She had to keep her cool. Wilson was watching.

"So," she said. "We have strong reason to believe you were the one orchestrating the drug-smuggling operation. You'll make it easier on all of us by admitting to it. The DA is willing to consider making a deal with you. Best-case scenario without that deal, Mr. Hakonson, is you're facing a lifetime in prison."

"I didn't smuggle anything," Channing said.

"Mr. Hakonson," said Giana with a sweet smile. "Let me talk."

He sighed and leaned back. "I don't have anything to hide, Giana. I didn't do it."

"So you found drugs in the safe," said Giana to Ella. "But do you actually have proof that he put them there? Finger-prints? Video?" pressed Giana. "Anything?"

Ella narrowed her eyes. "It's Mr. Hakonson's private safe, so no one would be able to access it but him. But that's not even the point. What matters, Mr. Hakonson, is that all facts point to you. The biggest one..."

She removed the lab report from her file and moved the paper towards him and the lawyer. "...is the fact that we found traces of cocaine in building Mo5. The building that you claim you did not use for anything but sword-fighting practice. The cameras on the other warehouses are conveniently positioned at such angles that it's impossible to see who goes in or out of the building—the only building in the port you denied us access to until you felt cornered. Combined with the mysterious black cars that keep coming for you..."

She shifted a photo taken from security footage of the gate where Channing had been dumped out of the first black SUV. "The significant decrease in cocaine found through your port ever since you took over..."

She shifted another report towards them and pointed at a highlighted phrase. "And an affidavit from an FBI informant stating that someone at the top of the Port of Boston is responsible for large-scale cocaine trafficking."

"Ella," said Channing suddenly, quietly, and with heat in his voice. "Look at me."

She was looking at the paper. Not at him. Her heart beat so hard it hurt. He was about to betray her. He was about to tell everyone about their affair.

Her chest hurt as though her broken heart was pumping venom into her bloodstream. Wilson was watching behind that mirror. Ricardo's stare could pierce her.

"Mr. Hakonson—" she started.

"Ella, look at me."

"Mr. Hakonson," said Giana, concern palpable in her voice. "Please, let me talk to the detectives, for your own good."

"Ella!" he commanded.

She lifted her gaze. His eyes were almost black in the artificial light of the interrogation room, and so intense they set her on fire.

"I am not a drug trafficker," he said slowly.

He wanted to play this game? She'd show him how to play coy with her. Play and flirt and kiss and tell her this was just the beginning...

"The black SUV spitting you out beaten up, Mr. Hakonson. I witnessed that. Who was that? Who did that to you?"

He clenched his teeth. "I can't tell you that."

"My client reserves the right not to incriminate himself based on the Fifth Amendment," said the lawyer.

"I understand, but that doesn't help you. Let me explain how all that looks to us and to the DA. The port has been pretty much drug-free. A couple of batches were found but nothing major. Great. Everyone assumes you're doing a phenomenal job with port security, and every criminal is terrified to smuggle through the Port of Boston. Right? Okay. Then, a random scan does find over a thousand pounds of highest quality cocaine. So, who can this be? Cocaine is usually shipped from Colombia, so are Colombian crime organizations trying to interest new generations of consumers who don't want cheap crack? The Boston Mafia is well known to work heroin from the Middle East, so cocaine is typically not their product. Small street gangs in Boston aren't as strong as in other states. But this cocaine has been found on the streets for two years at least. So, who is behind it?"

She took a pen and tapped it on the table. Channing stared at her without moving, without blinking, though his jaw ticked under his short beard.

"Perhaps the one person who has access to everything that comes through the port," she said. "Someone who may have criminal connections."

She looked down at the table, then back up at him. "We know about the three men that attacked you and wounded you." Her voice wavered a little at the memory of suturing the wound on Channing's shoulder. "The strange wolf pack that appeared to protect you from those men and again at the port, which suggests that you have trained wild animals for exactly this purpose."

She turned the page in the folder and retrieved a photo. Channing's eyes fell on it. She saw the light of any hope die in them. Good. She got him. If there would be any confession from his side, it would be now.

She moved the photo towards him.

"You in a stereotypical dark alley, talking to a man known in the criminal world as Clicker. A man known for trafficking weapons. What, are you now into illegal guns, too?"

He inhaled deeply.

"Do not reply, Mr. Hakonson," said the lawyer. "None of this proves that he is responsible for the trafficking. Talking to a man in an alley proves nothing. The drugs could have been planted, even in his safe, and the drug trafficking could very well be organized without his knowledge and under his nose."

"He is still charged with possession," said Ricardo.

"For now," said Giana. "Any more questions?"

Channing started swaying a little. He looked even worse than he had when they'd started. Goddamn it, she couldn't hold him any longer. He needed help. Ella stared at the folder. "Only if your client will answer any of them."

"Great," said Giana. "Then we are leaving. You made bail, Mr. Hakonson."

He frowned. "What? Did you bail me out?"

"No."

"Then who?"

She whispered something in his ear, and if Ella had seen him shocked before, it was nothing compared to now. He looked like death itself had come to visit.

"Who bailed him out?" said Ella.

Giana stood up and gathered her documents.

Ella rose to her feet. "It's public knowledge. I will find out. Who bailed you out?"

He stood up, his face ashen. "Leonardo Esposito."

The Boston Mafia boss.

When Channing and his lawyer left, Ricardo's face was pure reproach. "Ella..."

"What the fuck was that?" thundered Wilson as he burst into the interrogation room. "You almost had him. Unbelievable, O'Connor!" He scoffed.

Ella straightened her shoulders. "I will get him, sir. This is not over."

TWENTY-FIVE

"Careful!" roared Channing.

The nuclear reactor, which had been flung into the air by a crane, bumped into the wall, the bang reverberating through Channing's chest.

"Don't fucking make a nuclear wasteland out of Boston," he growled.

Then he really would be the reason for Ragnarök.

"Sorry, boss!" called Munchie dressed in a yellow radiation protection suit as he peeked out of the cabin of the crane. The ceiling of the basement had been retracted, and the crane stood on the floor of the warehouse. Channing watched the twenty-foot-long cylinder glisten in the blinking LED lights. The dark night outside blackened the windows above them.

Channing stood down in the basement, his eyes hard on the nuclear reactor. If all went well, he might be able to go back to the Viking Age today.

Good fucking timing.

For the last three days, ever since he'd been released from the police station, the investigation had been taken to the next level. His employees were being interrogated, every crate and every shelf was being turned over and swept. The police were looking at hours of security footage.

And he was being followed.

He didn't know if it was Ella, but he hoped so. Just today, the police had finally left building M05 alone. By some miracle, they hadn't discovered the secret entrance, and Channing wasn't going to try his luck. If they wanted to pin this on him, they would.

So he had to get out of here.

Today.

Especially because his dear grandfather wouldn't hesitate to help the police.

He'd told Channing he would pin the drug trafficking on him, and he had. Who else could have planted the bag of cocaine in his office?

Georgina, also in a yellow suit, stood by his side, watching the reactor. "Please, calm down," she said. "If it does break, you won't even feel a thing when you die."

"Thanks, Georgina," he muttered. "Are you sure you got the coordinates right? Are you sending me to the right time and place?"

"The calculations all check out," she said. "So pretty sure."

"Pretty sure isn't good enough."

"Pretty sure is the best we have right now, Mr. Hakonson."

Channing growled out a long sigh. His wounds were still aching, though he did feel much better after a long sleep. The iron pills helped. He wasn't as weak anymore.

The reactor descended slowly, and Georgina and Channing went to bolt it in place.

"Fascinating, isn't it?" said Georgina. "Such a small thing and it could power up Boston."

"Or kill everyone in the city," said Channing.

She shook her head. "Oh, it can *kill* many more, so we do have to be very, very careful."

Munchie came down the stairs with a proud expression on his face. "Shall we plug this baby in?"

"Yes, we shall." She handed a third yellow suit to Channing. "Mr. Hakonson, you should also dress in one. This reactor has one-of-a-kind security and protection against radiation, but you never know."

Channing waved it off. "I just need to get going. How long will it take?"

"It will take a while for it to power up, though it's very fast compared to the older generations. I guess we'll see."

Channing paced around the lab. "Can I do something to help?"

"You can please not ask stupid questions," said Georgina.

"She doesn't mean to be an evil bitch, boss," Munchie said. "But if we screw something up, we're all dead, along with millions of people on the New England coast."

Channing frowned. "Since when do you protect Georgina?"

Munchie took a stepladder and put it by the wall of the reactor. He climbed the steps and opened a small door where he began fiddling with switches and buttons. "Georgina finally realized I'm the man for her."

Georgina scoffed as she went to the giant spindle and grasped a thick cable that protruded from the back of the machine. "Please," she said. "Let's not discuss our private business with Mr. Hakonson."

"Are you two dating?" Channing asked, astonished.

"He's asking, hon," said Munchie.

Channing chuckled and crossed his arms over his chest.

"Odin's fart, I don't know what's more astonishing, you calling Georgina hon or Georgina not giving you crap for that."

"Munchie, I told you not to share our personal business," she said.

"There we go." Channing sighed.

They worked for a while, arguing about the order of where things had to be connected and how to do so. Three hours passed, and Channing kept wondering if he truly had managed to arrange everything before his departure. Would this really work?

Was he really about to leave?

Would he really never see Ella again?

As long as he did arrive in the ninth century and in the right year, he'd find his way back to his family and would save their lives. He'd live with them. Being who he was supposed to be.

A Viking.

A warrior.

But apart from the woman he was falling for. The only woman who made him feel like home was possible here.

Ella.

How the fuck could he leave her? Never see her again? Never touch her? Kiss her? Smell her hair?

The thought made him want to take a hammer, break the spindle, and fill the basement with concrete forever.

But he couldn't. He'd put so much at stake for this day. What could he tell her that would change her mind? How could he prove that he wasn't a drug smuggler?

He imagined for a moment that he could stay and fight for her. He could bring evidence against his grandfather; he could work with the police.

He could even confess to owning the nuclear reactor and take whatever punishment was coming. For her, he would do anything.

No. For the hundredth time, no. His family needed him.

After what felt like an eternity, Munchie closed a small, rectangular lid in the wall of the generator and stepped away from the twenty-foot-high metallic cylinder. It was about six feet in diameter and had a cone-shaped roof and a thin white staircase. It looked like a very small rocket. Thick black cables were plugged into it at the back.

"I believe this is done, boss," said Munchie. "We can start it."

Channing stood completely still. "Are you sure?"

"I'm sure, Mr. Hakonson," said Georgina, moving to the control panel of the machine, which showed an array of numbers, gauges, buttons, and switches. "The question is, are you ready?"

Channing wasn't. Giana had all the documents needed to divide and donate his estate. He'd also collected evidence against the Boston Mafia and his grandfather that would prove he had nothing to do with the drug smuggling and would allow Ella to arrest the man who was really responsible. So, all was done. And he could go home.

Only, his feet didn't move.

"I'm ready," he said, but even his voice sounded like he was lying.

"Okay," said Georgina. "Then get in place so you can touch the spindle."

"Right."

Channing picked up the bag he'd prepared to take with him. Viking clothes, food, silver, jewelry, antibiotics, and other medicine, which he knew his mother would appreciate, as well as books. He wasn't just bringing useful books with him, he brought children's books and a couple of mystery novels, and a romance novel that he thought she might like. For his father, he brought a chess game, and for his sister, a real mirror—a good one, with a perfect reflection. For his brother, he was bringing a couple of comic books. He also brought three paper notebooks and good pencils. Paper didn't exist in the ninth century, only expensive and rare vellum, which could only be obtained in the British Isles and through trade with Christian countries. His mother would love to draw and write, and maybe make notes for herself as she healed people and discovered more and more how different plants worked. He also brought a book about herbalism for her.

And, against his better judgment, he brought a photo of Ella. A small photo he'd downloaded from social media and printed out—to look at it and remember her, and know that over a thousand years later, she'd be born, and hopefully live happily.

Georgina pressed several buttons. A low noise came from the reactor, like a deep drill that had started somewhere far away.

"Ha!" cried Munchie as he opened a bag of chips.

The low buzz grew louder and louder. Channing exchanged a look with Munchie.

"Does this sound right?"

Munchie frowned. "Since it's one of three seventh-generation nuclear reactors in the world, I've never heard one work before. But something doesn't"—he came closer—"sound right."

Something within the reactor banged against its walls. It roared like a kitchen mixer. Georgina shook her head, her eyes huge. "Turn it off! This is—"

An object flew past her, nearly missing her head. It hit the wall. Then another one—brown and papery—flew past Channing.

"The fuck?" said Munchie as two, three, five, ten more brown things flew in all directions. Then the machine made a popping noise, and white powder thick as fog burst out of the reactor's top.

Dozens and dozens of packs wrapped in brown bags were flying around the secret basement. The lab looked as wintery as the city of Boston, white mist hanging in the air and slowly settling to the floor.

"Don't fucking breathe," said Channing. "It's cocaine."

"Cocaine is right," said a voice high above.

Channing looked up.

A group of men stood lined along the opening to the basement. His grandfather was among them, in an elegant camel-colored woolen coat, his white hair impeccable. Dozens of guns were pointed at Channing, one of them by Clicker. Next to his grandfather stood Peter van Beek, his face a stern mask, his deep, piggy eyes like two dark coals.

TWENTY-SIX

"Do switch off that thing," said Leonardo Esposito as he descended the stairs.

"What the fuck did you do?" roared Channing.

Leonardo's shoes clunked against the metal stairs. "And try not to breathe much. It might cloud your judgment and make you act strangely."

"Get out of my building," said Channing. Leonardo reached the bottom and stood in front of him. Piggy-eyed Peter followed him, his arms crossed over his chest.

Leonardo looked around with curiosity. "I will. As soon as we get our delivery."

"Were you in on this all along?" Channing asked Peter.

Standing next to Leonardo, Peter shrugged one shoulder. "How do you think there was so little smuggling caught?"

Channing clenched his fists, looking for something to hit. How could he be so naive? Ella was right. His improved security measures had nothing to do with the low rate of smuggled goods. "You fucking bastard."

Pete laid his hand on the gun tucked into his belt. "Maybe I am a fucking bastard. But I'm also a rich one. My girls are going to go to MIT and to Harvard. No port manager's salary could ever make that happen. And you never even realized we were using your precious building for it."

As more and more Mafia men were pouring into the basement lab, Channing's mind raced. How would he stop them? The amount of drugs that would flood Boston from this would result in a wave of new addicts who would try to find an escape from the *Fimbulwinter*, from hunger, and from violence.

He took a step forward, and the Mafia guys held to their guns. "So you chose to get thousands of people high? Chose to make them addicts? Chose to sink the economy of this country and support crime?"

Leonardo walked leisurely through the cocaine mist towards the spindle. "And what are you doing with this?" He wiped a thin layer of white powder off the golden surface with his hand. "Is this gold?"

Channing's jaw tightened. "That is none of your business."

"Mr. Hakonson believes in science," said Georgina.

Munchie nodded. "We're about to make a breakthrough. We already proved time travel is real."

"Shut up, you two," said Channing. The cocaine must be getting to them, loosening their tongues.

Leonardo laughed. "Is that what you chose to spend your millions on? Time travel?"

Yeah, you piece of shit. Because your goddamn son couldn't keep his violent hands off my mother.

If only you knew time travel brought your son's killer to this century...

Still chuckling, Leonardo picked up one of the brown packs and turned it in his hand. Then he threw it into the hands of one of his goons and made a gesture with his head, signaling for them to start picking up the bags.

Most of white mist has already settled by then, covering the concrete floor with a thin layer that looked like flour.

Munchie exchanged a glance with Georgina. "Aren't you afraid they're radioactive? You're going to sell radioactive cocaine on the streets? Do you know what kind of health problems that will cause? A really serious health crisis, that's what. Masses sick with cancer, radiation sickness..."

The men froze. One of them dropped the pack on the floor.

"Don't listen to him," Leonardo said to his men. "We took precautions. The cocaine is fine."

"If you say so, boss," said the man who dropped the pack. He picked it up and resumed gathering the packs.

"I wish you'd considered working with me instead of doing this." Leonardo nodded towards the spindle. "We could have made so much money, built a beautiful organization. And now..."

He waved his hand, and Clicker pointed a gun at Channing's head.

"Now I have to kill you."

"Don't kill him!" called Munchie. "He was about to go through time. He'll disappear anyway."

Leonardo shook his head. "Is that supposed to be a scientist? He's not very smart, is he?"

Clicker released the safety of the gun. Channing froze. Yet again he was looking death in the face. He'd been so close to going back.

No. He wouldn't let this criminal have power over his destiny. He wouldn't let anyone decide when he lived or when he died. Channing tensed, ready to attack.

"Police! Do not move!" called a voice from above.

He looked up. And there she was, gorgeous, her hair shining like gold under the lights, her cheeks rosy from the cold. She was pointing her gun at Clicker. More police were around her, everyone pointing guns at the Mafia men in the lab.

"Put your weapons down!" she cried. "Now!"

The Mafia men looked at their boss, who growled.

"Ella, do not shoot, it's a nuclear reactor," said Channing.

Her eyes widened.

Clicker turned to her and shot.

The Mafia men dropped the cocaine and started spilling around the lab, hiding behind the spindle, the reactor, and the tables. The police shot back, the room filling with the *pop-pop-pops* of gunfire. Channing ducked behind the spindle, taking Munchie and Georgina with him.

"You okay?" he asked them.

"Yes," said Georgina. Munchie nodded.

"Good lord, boss, you don't have a lot of friends, do you?"

Channing shook his head. "You have no idea. Can you send me now?"

A bullet ricocheted off the spindle.

"They really must stop, or we'll have a nuclear explosion in Boston!" cried Georgina.

"Goddamn it," spat Channing. "Just start it. I'll make sure no one else goes."

"All right." Crouching, Georgina crawled to the control panel. Staying low, she began to punch the buttons and manage the controls.

He peered from behind the spindle. Several of the police officers were down—wounded or killed—and his eyes darted, frantically looking for Ella. They must have called for backup. When would it be here?

The police were descending the stairs. Ella was among them.

He had to help. He crawled to the Mafia guy who was shooting from behind an overturned table. Channing punched him, and the guy dropped the gun. With another blow to the guy's head, he knocked him unconscious. He turned and shot at another Mafia goon who had his gun on Ella.

Ella and the three officers were still making their way down. With horror, he saw her clutching at her shoulder under the Kevlar vest. That had been too close.

"Fuck it," he spat and shot another one of Leonardo's guys in the shoulder.

Ella and her colleagues had reached the basement and were hiding behind cupboards and tables, shooting.

Leonardo was hiding behind an overturned table with Clicker and another man by his side.

"Clear the goddamn way!" roared Leonardo, pushing one of his bodyguards forward. The man jumped from behind the table, and with surprisingly good aim, shot the three cops. They fell with grunts of pain.

"Ella..." Channing mumbled as he moved towards her, ready to throw himself on her to cover her if need be.

But the shots subsided, and the Mafia men ran towards the stairs, covering Leonardo. They didn't even bother about the cocaine.

"Go, you fools," roared Leonardo.

Peter ran with them.

With his stomach dropping, Channing reached Ella. She lay under one of her colleagues. He pushed the dead body off her.

With a cold, slippery coil in his stomach, Channing looked her over. She had the graze on her shoulder but looked fine otherwise. He touched her neck, searching for her pulse.

It was there.

"Ella," he said as he took her into his arms.

Then he saw it—blood at the back of her skull. She must

have hit her head as she fell under the weight of her colleague, who'd died protecting her.

Just as Channing would have done.

Lying in his arms, she opened her eyes. "What—" she mumbled.

"You're okay. You're safe," Channing said. "Is backup on the way?"

"Yes. The SWAT team."

"They should follow the Mafia. They just escaped."

"Goddamn it," she said it weakly, and the weight of her— light and sweet—felt so right in his arms.

"I'll call 911," he said. "Don't move."

But of course she moved. She sat up.

"Is she okay, boss?" said Munchie.

"She's fine. Keep working. Tell me when I can go."

"Sure thing," said Munchie.

"Go where?" Ella looked around.

Channing clenched his jaw. "You know where."

She blinked, staring at the golden spindle behind him with confusion. "Is that..."

"The time machine. Yeah."

Her eyes widened at the spindle and the control panel. Munchie and Georgina were pressing buttons, exchanging brief questions and replies that were meant to coordinate tasks between them.

"These are the two MIT scientists who built it. Dr. Miles Mochizuki and Dr. Georgina Brandon. The Mafia were the real smugglers. They and my port manager, Peter van Beek, have been smuggling drugs into the States for years, it seems."

"You were telling the truth," she whispered, her eyes wet and shiny. "You didn't betray me... You're not a criminal..."

Relief flooded him. He'd wanted so much for her to know he was innocent.

"I'm not."

Their eyes locked, and it was as though a dam had broken between them, a dam of misunderstanding, a dam of mistrust.

With a tear crawling down her face, Ella reached out to him and kissed him. Her lips were salty, warm, and wet, and the kiss was hard, full of relief and passion and promise.

It felt like it lasted an eternity but was likely just a second or two—that would be all they'd ever have—and when she broke the kiss off, hard reality swarmed around him.

The nuclear reactor and the time travel machine that was waiting for him. That was all he'd been living for for years.

Wounded and dead people were lying around, both Mafia and police. The floor was covered in white powder, blood, and splintered wood from tables and cupboards riddled with bullet holes. The spindle had scratches on the surface, but was otherwise intact.

"You need to sit," Channing said. "Don't move until the ambulance comes."

"I don't care about the ambulance," she groaned, looking at the fallen officers. "That could have been me..."

And I would have died with you...

Channing glanced back at the spindle. Sirens wailed somewhere in the distance. If the police came here now, there wouldn't be another chance to go. They'd see the nuclear reactor. They'd have questions. Perhaps he'd be cleared of the drug-smuggling charges, but he'd be charged with smuggling nuclear material.

He had to go.

Now.

He looked over his shoulder at the two figures in protective gear leaning over the control panel. "Is it ready?"

"Almost!" said Georgina as she typed something into the computer connected to the panel. "Get ready."

The spindle began spinning. Glowing, golden strings began rolling around it like giant lassos, meeting, circling. The room filled with a golden glow so bright Channing had to narrow his eyes to look at it.

"Now!" cried Georgina. "Year: 896. Place: near Lomdalen, Norway. The coordinates are in. I don't think it will hold for long."

Ella rose to her feet, astonishment written on her face. "You're not serious."

Channing went to the spindle and picked up the backpack he'd prepared. There it was, the golden surface. He could just reach out and lay his hand on it, and he'd be gone from this world. He'd be back with his family. Fourteen years all for this moment. Every single penny he'd earned, every single word he'd said, every single action he'd taken was for this.

But his hand wouldn't move.

He looked back at her. So beautiful his breath caught, with her hair golden, and wide blue eyes burning like two sapphires. Was there truly no chance for them? Could he really go into the world where she didn't exist?

Could he leave the woman he loved forever?

He had to.

For his family.

He turned to the spindle, his fist clenching and unclenching as he told himself to bring his hand up and press it against the surface.

"Do not move," said a familiar voice from behind.

Channing froze, then looked back.

Eirik, Ragnar, and Náli surrounded Ella. She was tight in Náli's grip, and Eirik's ax was pressed against her throat.

TWENTY-SEVEN

"Boss! Now or never!" cried Munchie. "We're losing the threads."

"Fucking hell," cursed Channing.

"Mr. Hakonson!" called Georgina.

Ella jerked in Náli's arms. "Let me go, you bastard."

Náli tightened his grip. "Shut up."

Channing couldn't go through time, not when Ella was in the hands of his enemies, with a blade at her throat.

Eirik gave an evil smirk. "Finally, we could break through the wolves. It is as though they want Ragnarök to happen. Loki's spawn, hey?"

Damn it. He was right. Everything was pointing towards Ragnarök more and more.

Eirik looked at Ella. "And now, old friend, you're finally vulnerable."

Channing raised his hand in a placating gesture. "Let her go," he said. "You need me." He turned to Munchie and Georgina. "You guys should leave. The police are coming. I want you out of here. The moment I distract them, run. Understood?"

Munchie shook his head. "We can't leave you—"

"Understood?" Channing pressed.

"Yes, Mr. Hakonson," said Georgina.

Slowly, he walked to Eirik.

"I said, let her go."

Channing put his backpack down and undid his sword from it. "You want to kill me, here I am."

He stood with his sword, his heart thumping as it did before every battle. Despite the ache in his shoulder and his side, he lifted his sword high with both hands, ready to attack.

Ragnar slashed with his ax and Channing deflected it, then he stepped in and smashed his sword's pommel into the warrior's face. Ragnar yelled, staggering back. Immediately, Channing whirled away from Náli's ax. He spun in a 360-degree turn and slashed him in the side, but Náli was right on time and deflected the sword.

With a grunt, Ragnar launched at him again, slamming into Channing like a battering ram, and he flew back, landing by the spindle. Only a few inches separated him from the glaring, spinning gold. The moving threads crackled by his ear.

He gathered his strength and stood up, and was kicked back by Ragnar's head connecting with his solar plexus. Ragnar rammed him right into the table, and the sharp edge of the tabletop dug painfully into his kidneys. His sword fell.

Fuck.

He kneed Ragnar in the stomach, and the man gasped. That was the moment Channing needed. He pushed the man back, leaned down, picked up his sword, and in one diagonal slash aiming for the neck, cut the man's head clean off.

A combined gasp from the twenty-first-century people made him realize this was his first kill in fourteen years.

He wasn't used to fighting with swords anymore. And killing was something he'd never enjoyed as a Viking, but now he was truly sorry to take another life. Even though it was to protect himself and the woman he loved.

Eirik stared at him with astonished, bewildered, and crazed eyes. Náli gave out an outraged, pained cry, like an animal. "You fucking killed Ragnar!" he roared.

He held his sword in both hands so hard, Channing saw his knuckles whiten. "There are no gods in this world," Náli growled, his eyes so dark and so full of hatred, they were almost black. "He didn't go to Valhalla."

Channing gripped his own sword and placed it by his ear, ready for the attack. "Neither will you."

He said it, but did he really mean it? Would he really be able to kill Eirik when it came to it?

He didn't know.

For now, he had no choice but to fight.

He attacked. Step, two, three, and a downward slash aiming at the man's head. His blow was deflected, the kickback of metal against metal resonating in his bone marrow. Muscle memory from his daily fighting practice since he was eight kicked in.

But Náli had more experience. He'd been living in the Viking Age far longer than Channing. He was stronger, and soon he was the one who had started attacking. *Thrust, slash, thrust, slash, kick.* The room was filled with the rhythmic ring of metal against metal along with the crackling of the golden threads around the spindle.

Channing was backing up as Náli's powerful thrusts fell on him, feeling as if Náli was wielding a sledgehammer, not a sword.

Use your strength, he remembered his father's words as he trained him in sword and ax fighting. *Every warrior has*

*strengths and weaknesses. You have them, too. Use your
strengths to cover for your weaknesses.*

So where Channing couldn't win with strength, he had to
use speed. He had been jogging daily; he could move fast. So
when Náli raised his sword over his head with both his arms,
Channing ducked low to the ground and thrust his sword into
the man's abdomen. The blade sank into the hard flesh with
difficulty, and Náli's face crumpled in a silent grimace of shock
and pain.

As Channing drew the bloodied sword back, Náli fell to his
side holding the gaping chasm in his stomach.

He locked his eyes with Channing. *"You* should die. Not
the world. Not the gods. Not thousands of people. You."

A chill ran down Channing's spine. They had to be wrong.
How could he be the reason for Ragnarök? He wasn't a
witcher, and he wasn't a priest close to the gods. Was it
somehow connected to the fact that he had been born to a time
traveler? That although he had been conceived in the twenty-
first century, he was born in the ninth? Had his very existence
endangered the world?

Would Ragnarök really stop if Channing died? Maybe he
should just let Eirik kill him.

No. Maybe he was too much of a coward.

Or maybe, there were still people he loved too much.

People he had to protect.

Panting, Channing looked at Eirik, who growled as he saw
the death of his other sword-brother.

Eirik pushed Ella aside, gripped his sword, and ran at
Channing like an enraged bull, slashing at Channing's shoulder. Channing barely managed to step aside and pushed Eirik,
who was practically flying past him. Channing staggered and
almost hit the spindle, but managed to stop himself at the last
minute.

Eirik turned with an expression of battle rage. There was no stopping him now. He'd kill Channing. There was no remorse, no sadness, no anything in his eyes. Only the pure decisiveness of a fanatic with a death wish.

With his sword raised, he walked towards Channing like a machine, unapologetic, with one aim that was clear in his eyes: kill Channing Hakonson or die trying.

He raised his sword higher and delivered a strike so powerful, he forced Channing's sword down, and his blade might have left an indent in Channing's. He kept pressing, striking at Channing over and over like a blacksmith, the blows ringing off Channing's sword as he met each hit. Channing remembered distantly how Eirik had always had great upper body strength. His shoulder muscles seemed to have been made of iron, his bones as strong as rocks.

Channing's arms absorbed the impact of the attack, his own bones vibrating. He wouldn't have the advantage of speed as he'd had against Náli—Eirik was the most perfect warrior Channing had ever known, both strong and quick.

He'd been Father's most treasured warrior. Hakon had often said if Eirik went to Valhalla, he'd be Odin's favorite.

Channing had always felt he was lucky to fight alongside this man, but now he was on the receiving end of his skill.

Channing twisted out of Eirik's sword's path, and struck at his unprotected side, but Eirik jumped away in time. That gave Channing an advantage, and he started his own attack. He thrust his sword towards the man's abdomen, but Eirik deflected it.

Then, with lightning-fast speed, he thrust his sword down from above, and Channing fell for it. He put his sword up in a protective movement, leaving the lower part of his body vulnerable.

Eirik's eyes glinting with victory, he thrust his sword up from below and straight towards Channing's unprotected gut.

There wouldn't be an escape this time.

He'd lost.

A loud bang sounded, and Eirik was knocked back and to the side. Channing turned to see Ella standing with her gun in both hands.

Another shot came but a stiff, metallic ring meant she'd missed. She fired again.

And hit Eirik straight on.

He stared astounded at Ella, then he fell, blood blooming on his chest and shoulder.

"Stop Ragnarök..." he whispered and then went still, his eyes glossy.

Channing looked at Ella, who was staring at Eirik and panting, her gun still in her hands. She turned back to Channing, eyes wide, and wild, and blinking. Slowly, she tucked the gun back into her holster and walked to him, looking a little bewildered, like she couldn't feel the ground under her feet.

When she stood by Channing's side, she looked at Eirik again. "I killed him..." she whispered. "I'm supposed to be protecting lives, and I killed him..."

Silence fell over them, and Channing wanted to reach out and pat her shoulder soothingly, take her pain away. But that silence...

The threads of time had stopped crackling.

He glanced at the spindle.

It stood unmoving. There was no glow. There was nothing.

Bullet holes in the gold told him everything. By saving him, Ella had damaged the time machine. She'd destroyed his only chance to get back to his family and save their lives. His mother, his father, his sister, and his brother—the latter two were completely innocent in all of this. They didn't deserve to die so young in a fire.

None of his family did.

She looked at him, her eyes still wide and now filling with tears. "I killed him."

"I killed two men, too, just now. Will you arrest me?"

He saw the truth in her eyes. If she arrested him, she could get out of this. She'd have the case closed because the bad guy would be behind bars.

Somewhere in the distant silence, police sirens were blaring, coming closer. She looked up at him.

He cupped her jaw. "Odin and Thor, I'm so glad you're alive, my love."

There they were, the two words his heart had felt for days... perhaps ever since he saw her for the first time.

My love.

He loved her.

She inhaled sharply, and their gazes locked.

"Your *love*?" she whispered.

He sighed out a long, tortured breath. Did it change anything?

"You have the power to stop me now, to arrest me, Ella. For smuggling the nuclear reactor. For killing these men. But I need to return to my family, to the ninth century. I need to save their lives."

Her nostrils flared as she wiped away her tears. "What about *my* family?" She waved her arm around. "What about saving my disabled father's life and my brother with special needs?"

She marched two angry steps towards the spindle. "What about my baby niece and another one on the way?" She waved her arm in a wide arc. "This thing seems to be the answer to so many of your problems. People shouldn't be able to travel in time to resolve their issues. You should accept your destiny. Take action to improve life where you are. Stay here, with me. Let's figure out how to get through this together."

She slammed her fist against the gold. "If I traveled in time—"

The machine whirred and buzzed. The engraved Norse runes and curved patterns glowed and exploded in a burst of pure light. Golden threads of time crackled and grew and spun around the spindle as though some giant invisible hand was working it. For a split second, the light from the patterns and the runes and the threads intensified into a single flash and blinded Channing.

He had to close his eyes, and when he opened them...

She was gone.

Then several things happened at once. Many footsteps sounded somewhere high above, making Channing look up.

Ricardo stood at the edge of the entrance to the basement, his gun pointed at Channing. He was staring at the place where Ella had just disappeared.

"Where the fuck did she go?" he yelled, then his eyes locked on Channing. "What did you do to her?"

Channing ran to the spindle. Maybe it did work, after all.

"Freeze!" yelled Ricardo. "Or I will shoot! Hands up!"

"Do not move!" yelled another cop. Channing froze and raised his hands.

"Throw your sword on the floor!" yelled Ricardo, his feet pounding down the metallic stairs as he descended.

He did, and the bloody sword clanked against the floor.

"Channing Hakonson," yelled Ricardo as he was coming closer, "you're under arrest. You have the right to remain silent." He reached Channing and drew his arms behind his back. "Anything you say can and will be used against you in a court of law..."

The cool metal of the handcuffs burned the skin of his wrists.

As Ricardo led Channing up the stairs from the basement, he growled in his ear, "You dickhead, you will answer for this. You will tell me where she is, and you will be locked up for this for life. We have enough proof now."

And while he was being led out of the basement and away from his chance to go back in time, all Channing could think about was Ella. Where was she? If she had traveled back in time, he had to do everything in his power to go after her.

Whenever she was.

———

NORWAY, 896

ELLA OPENED her eyes to a gray light that was painful after complete darkness. She was lying on rocks on the top of a mountain, and the view that spread before her took her breath away.

A long body of water curled around the base of the mountains. It was too broad and still to be a river. The mountains were so steep and tall, they looked like granite walls with their tops in snow. Sparse vegetation—trees and bushes and grass—grew on the low coast by the water.

There were ships—wooden ships, each with a single, square sail and a high, curved bow with some sort of dragon figureheads...

Viking?

Her heart slammed hard. Where was snowed-in Boston? Where was Channing Hakonson? The time machine?

The goddamn time machine—she'd touched it, and the last

thing she remembered were the golden threads that had pulled her somewhere, tearing her apart on a molecular level. Reality had blurred and paused and shifted just like in her dreams.

"And who would you be, pretty one?"

A male voice came from behind her. She turned around.

A man, big and muscular, with a mane of red hair and a long red beard stood looming over her, one hand holding an ax, and a round shield visible behind his back.

Norse tattoos covered the side of his face. He was dressed in a rough tunic, and a brown fur cloak covered his shoulders. Behind him were men armed with axes, swords, and spears, some on horses, all dressed like this man.

Like Eirik, Náli, and Ragnar.

And he spoke Old Norse.

A tremor shook Ella as fear crawled into her gut like an icy snake. Slowly, she got to her feet and pointed the gun at the man. Her hands shook.

"What year is it?" she said.

He frowned, looking at the gun in her hands with acute curiosity.

"An average year, so far. Summer has been warm but rainy."

Goddamn it. Vikings probably didn't calculate years, especially not based on when Christ was born.

"Who are you?"

Her hands shook. "Who are you?"

"Harald, King of Norway. And what is that you're holding in your hands?"

No, no, no! Please, let her not have traveled into the ninth century instead of Channing!

King Harald took a tentative step towards her. "Do not move! I'll shoot you!"

The man chuckled. "Shoot me? With that?"

With a smirk, he marched towards her. Before she could think, she pulled the trigger, once, twice, three times...

But only clicks came out of it. Empty. She'd emptied it in the goddamn lab.

King Harald reached her, and before she could react, gave her a hard slap, so painful her ears rang and her head spun. She assumed a fighting position, but her wooziness made her disoriented. She made a few jabs at King Harald, but he only laughed. He gave a sign and men came to her, locking her arms behind her back. She stomped on their feet, but they only grunted in pained amusement, as though she were a child trying to fight adults.

"You're a pretty, feisty little thing, aren't you?" said King Harald. "And where did you come from?" He narrowed his blue eyes at her. "Did one of the Norns send you to me?" He looked her up and down. "Good. A time traveler. A beautiful woman with the spirit of a Valkyrie. A woman of my heart. You'll come with me. I am in need of a wife. We'll get along just fine."

He turned around and gave a gesture to follow him. But before she could tell him to go fuck himself, a dirty hand covered her mouth and she was dragged after King Harald.

Ella screamed and tried to bite the hand, beating against the men that held her, but it seemed her destiny was sealed.

She was in the ninth century, Viking Scandinavia when her family and Channing—everyone she loved—were in the future, left in a dying world.

She had to get back there to help them. And she would... whatever it took...

THANK you for reading AGE OF WOLVES. I hope you loved the delicate beginnings of Channing and Ella's story. Find out what happens next when Ella needs to decide between her heart and her duty in AGE OF ICE.

READ AGE OF ICE now >
⭐⭐⭐⭐⭐ "Omg...I am in awe of this book. The book and the series are simply amazing!"

SIGN-UP FOR MY NEWSLETTER to find out when new books release, hear about exclusive giveaways, and take a sneak peek into my future books.

FANCY A VIKING?
And other mysterious matchmakers are sending modern-day people to the Viking Age, too. If you haven't read Holly and Einar's story yet, be sure to pick up VIKING'S DESIRE - and get to know more of Channing's backstory across the CALLED BY A VIKING series.
A captive time traveler. A Viking jarl on a mission. Will marriage be the price of her freedom?

READ VIKING'S DESIRE now >
⭐⭐⭐⭐⭐ "Fabulous! What a great way to start a new series!"

OR STAY with Channing and Ella's story and keep reading for an excerpt from AGE OF ICE...

YOUR BONUS: A GLIMPSE INTO AGE OF ICE

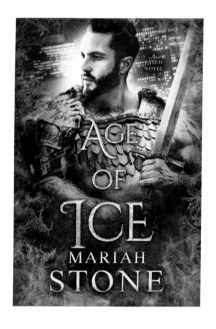

Chapter 1

Norway, 896

The shed reeked of old fish. They must have cleaned out herring and salmon guts here, Ella thought, right on that massive wooden table. Even in semidarkness, scales stuck to the scarred surface glimmered dully with silver and mother-of-pearl.

The only light came during the day. Dust danced in the sun rays seeping through the uneven slits between the poorly constructed wall planks and falling on the only three pieces of furniture. One, Ella's amazing bed, otherwise known as a heap of straw in the corner. Two, the aforementioned stinking table standing against the opposite wall. Three, a stool with three uneven legs.

During the three days that she'd been trapped here, she'd tried to move the table so that it stood next to the door. Her plan had been to climb on top of it and attack the guard or King Harald himself. That was pretty much her only chance to escape since her gun and her bulletproof Kevlar vest had been taken away from her.

But the damn table was like a boulder and just wouldn't budge.

There were no windows, not even a floor—just cold, packed dirt—and plenty of gaps in the walls.

And there was the door.

Her only way out.

Her only way to go back to her own time…or at least a chance to find out how to return home. Because she wasn't even entirely sure how she'd ended up here in the first place. All she knew was that one moment she'd been in the Port of Boston, standing in a warehouse among dozens of wounded and dead bodies, cocaine bags, and a giant golden spindle that was a broken time machine.

The man she was falling for had just told her two things. He'd called her his love.

And he'd told her he'd smuggled a goddamn nuclear reactor to power the time machine.

She'd gotten mad at him. She'd said things... She'd touched the golden spindle and...*poof*.

When she'd opened her eyes, she'd been standing on a cliff overlooking a Norwegian fjord. And King Harald and a band of his Viking warriors had immediately taken her captive.

Ella pressed her face to a slit between the planks. Even through the gap, she could see the breathtaking, rough beauty of the place.

The village was on the shore of a fjord, a long, narrow inlet flanked by mountains and cliffs that shot up like granite walls, so high they could support the sky.

The houses themselves were all made of timber. None of them had windows and all of them had thatched roofs with carved dragon gables. Most of the women were blonde and wore apron dresses, and the men wore linen and woollen tunics and some sort of baggy trousers and patched shoes.

Goats, sheep, chickens, and geese walked around. Dogs barked, children ran and played. Men cut firewood, carried buckets of water, dressed fish and game. Women were mostly indoors, no doubt cooking, though Ella saw several sweep and clean, take out buckets with food waste for the pigs and cows, and run after the children. She heard everything from outside the shed really well, and still didn't know how she could understand Old Norse without ever learning it.

There was always a guard by her door, one of the Viking warriors. She'd seen them when they opened the door and let the slave girl, Ciara, in to bring her food and take her night pot out.

King Harald himself hadn't come to see her yet, and she'd overheard people talking, saying he was away.

She'd like to punch Harald in the face. How long was he

intending to keep her here—and why? Harald was the one who had sent those Viking assassins after Channing through time...

Channing...

How could a single word send a stabbing pain through her, as though a needle pierced right through the middle of her chest?

Every single doubt about him had vanished. He'd been telling the truth this whole time.

Time travel was real.

Any thoughts she'd had about this being a trick had been wiped away by the three days she'd spent observing people, listening to conversations about raids, fishing, the harvest. About the blacksmith being too cocky and asking prices that were too high—two sacks of barley for a sword. The worries about an unknown illness that had made an old man weak and double up in pain. How a woman had lost her baby in childbirth, but thankfully, was alive herself.

The talk about making mead, and the blot—a ritual sacrifice of a sheep on one of the rune rocks—that was planned for King Harald's return.

At first, she'd thought this might be some sort of reenactment game...a role play...some secluded community that had gone hardcore on the whole "let's live in the past" thing.

But she wasn't even in the United States anymore.

Channing had been telling the truth... He had been just trying to get back to the age where he belonged.

This age.

The wrong age for her.

She had to find a way back to the twenty-first century.

Time stretched and crawled, endless and merciless. On the fourth day, horse hooves and heavy steps sounded from the outside. Many excited voices approached, and then the door opened, letting direct sunlight in shielded by several tall, broad-shouldered, muscular frames.

She jumped to her feet, her knees bent, her fists clenched, ready to fight if she needed to.

One of the shadows entered, and as he stepped inside, she noticed his red hair and beard, his handsome, intelligent face. King Harald.

"Stay back," he threw over his shoulder. "She is not a threat to me."

He was wearing a long bear-fur hide on his shoulders that gave him even more mass and presence. He turned back and, using his ax, pushed the door closed.

Why were all these men so huge? Channing was big, but many men in the village looked like they had tree trunks for arms and boulders for shoulders. Must be all the longship rowing. Even the king looked like a weathered warrior.

Well, he clearly wore more expensive outfits. The bear cloak was probably special, and she wondered if he had hunted the animal himself. And he wore silver chains and a thick torc—a large, rigid ring made of silver strands twisted together—around his neck.

And then there was this look in his eyes. She'd seen it many times. All men in power had it. That calm, contained arrogance, the sense that they owned everything. Channing had it, too, only behind it, there was a big, kind heart and an unbendable sense of honor.

Harald turned to her and looked her up and down, then put his ax into the belt around his waist. "So. Gods sent you to me through time."

She raised one eyebrow. "Not sure about the 'gods' part, but definitely through time. And you will help me to go back."

He chuckled and little wrinkles formed around his eyes. "I will do no such thing, woman."

Anger that she'd been containing for the past three days started boiling somewhere deep in her guts. "How dare you." Her voice came out low, but the smirk in his eyes was gone as he, no doubt, heard the steel beneath her words.

"How dare I?" He walked farther into the shed, the streams of sunlight sparkling off his chain mail under his bear skin. "I am king. I am the favorite of the gods. I dare everything."

He stopped before the pile of hay in the corner.

"You cocky son of a bitch. You know that what you did was kidnapping, a punishable offense in my time. Had you done that in Boston, you'd be in jail faster than you could take your next breath."

Harald cocked one brow, amusement returning into his gaze. "I do not know what a jail is or a punishable offense, but I like the fire in you, woman."

"Stop calling me 'woman,'" she growled.

"Are you not a woman?" His gaze went up and down her body, and Ella stopped a shiver of disgust.

"I am, but that doesn't make any difference for—"

He crossed the distance between them in three steps. One moment, he was across the room, the next he was towering over her like a giant bear.

"Oh, Freya's tongue, it makes all the difference." He raised his hand and dragged his knuckle down her cheek. With her stomach in knots, Ella shook his hand off. All humor from his face gone, he grabbed her cheeks between his thumb and his index finger in a painful pinch, squishing her lips together. "The Norns send women across time to men so that they find love. Mia, Hakon Ulfson's wife, is a time traveler. There are others. I have concubines, slaves I use for pleasure. I have children, though currently not a wife. But I do not love any of them. Who is to say you were not sent here for me?"

A cold shiver swept through Ella. She was so far out of her

depth here. This time was so different. Women had fought for centuries for the right to be as independent as men, to be their equals.

The Viking Age was just at the beginning of that fight. Which meant, this jerk and other men like him treated women like property.

Oh, hell no. She wouldn't let anyone treat her with anything but respect, and she'd show him.

She stomped on his foot. He let go of her face and groaned in pain. Using his distraction, she threw her elbow back and drove her fist into his stomach, only to meet a steely wall of muscle. His next grunt sounded like a chuckle.

She'd show him.

"I'll teach you to treat women with respect."

Using his distraction, she kneed him right between the legs. He made a strange sound like a loud sigh and stepped back, doubling up and covering his groin.

"You bitch," he gave out.

"I am not a wallflower, nor a slave, nor an object of amusement for anyone, not even a king. I am a police officer, the daughter of a police officer, and I have a sick father, and a brother with special needs, and a whole family that depends on me. I eat scumbags like you for breakfast. And if you touch me like that ever again, next time your balls won't hurt because I kicked them, but because you'll be missing them."

Harald exhaled slowly and straightened himself. He must still be in a lot of pain behind the reddening stone mask of his face. Somewhere deep, a small voice told her she was probably wrong to make an enemy out of him. Told her she would be better off being sly and diplomatic.

He cleared his throat, his eyes fixed on her. "I will treat you with respect, woman. I always treat women with respect. You are no slave and you are a warrior woman, I see. But if you think I will back off, you are wrong. If anything, your strength and your beauty makes me want you more."

Her jaw must have hit the ground. "Why do you even need me? Why are you keeping me here?"

Slowly, he stepped towards her, his mouth tight in pain. "You are so beautiful..." he said, looking her face up and down. "It is hard to imagine Freya herself did not come down from Valhalla."

She swallowed, fighting the instinct to back away from him. When another Viking had towered over her like that, she'd wanted to kiss him, to hug him, to dissolve in his touch.

She wanted to run away from this man. "What do you want from me?"

"If you are from the future, you might have heard of Ulf Hakonson?"

He was speaking of Channing, using his Norse name, Ulf.

"Not just him. I know your goons, Eirik, Ragnar, and Náli."

His eyes didn't just widen, they sparkled. "Did Ulf's death save the world, just as the völva foretold?"

Her heart slammed against her ribs. She should think carefully, she should play this right. But the memory of the swords and axes flashing, hurting Channing, of her aiming her gun. Her bullet, piercing Eirik. The first life she'd ever taken. Blood flowing.

The cool, smooth surface of the time machine under her palm...and then nothing.

All because of him.

"No, you murderous bastard. Your assassins died. Ulf is still alive."

"And you saw all that?"

"Yes, I saw all that. I killed Eirik."

Harald's face relaxed in a serene, peaceful expression that made the skin on her back crawl. "Then the answer to your question of why you are here is clear, beautiful woman from the future."

"Oh yeah?" She didn't want to know the answer. She shouldn't ask, she shouldn't even bother. But like an idiot, she asked, "Why?"

"Because you will bring him to me. And when I kill him and stop Ragnarök, you will be mine."

Keep reading AGE OF ICE.

ALSO BY MARIAH STONE

Mariah's Time travel Romance Series

- CALLED BY A HIGHLANDER
- CALLED BY A VIKING
- CALLED BY A PIRATE
- FATED

Mariah's Regency Romance Series

- DUKES AND SECRETS

View all of Mariah's Books in Reading Order

Scan the QR code for the complete list of Mariah's ebooks, paperbacks, and audiobooks in reading order.

GET A FREE MARIAH STONE BOOK!

Join Mariah's mailing list to be the first to know of new releases, free books, special prices, and other author giveaways.

freehistoricalromancebooks.com

ENJOY THE BOOK? YOU CAN MAKE A DIFFERENCE!

Please, leave your honest review for the book.
As much as I'd love to, I don't have financial capacity like New York publishers to run ads in the newspaper or put posters in subway.

But I have something much, much more powerful!

Committed and loyal readers

If you enjoyed the book, I'd be so grateful if you could spend five minutes leaving a review on the book's Amazon page.

Thank you very much!

ABOUT MARIAH STONE

Mariah Stone is a bestselling author of time travel romance novels, including her popular Called by a Highlander series and her hot Viking, Pirate, and Regency novels. With nearly one million books sold, Mariah writes about strong modern-day women falling in love with their soulmates across time. Her books are available worldwide in multiple languages in e-book, print, and audio.

Subscribe to Mariah's newsletter for a free time travel romance book today at mariahstone.com/signup/!

facebook.com/mariahstoneauthor

instagram.com/mariahstoneauthor

bookbub.com/authors/mariah-stone

pinterest.com/mariahstoneauthor

amazon.com/Mariah-Stone/e/B07JVW28PJ

Made in United States
North Haven, CT
09 December 2024

62122204R00159